Children of the Dragon

Sliding one foot in front of the other, Daniel entered the river, pulling Max, then Lydia after him.

"Be careful!" he called. "The current is strong!"

The children were in midstream and the water was lapping at Max's waist when the torch began to flicker.

"Oh, no," whispered Lydia. She held the precious dragon egg more tightly.

Suddenly the darkness was shattered by a bellow. A huge head with tiny eyes and a great gaping mouth rose out of the water.

Max screamed and dropped the torch!

Children of the Dragon

by Rose Estes

illustrated by Carl Lundgren

RANDOM HOUSE   NEW YORK

Text copyright © 1985 by Rose Estes.
Illustrations copyright © 1985 by Carl Lundgren.
All rights reserved under International and Pan-American
Copyright Conventions. Published in the United States by
Random House, Inc., New York, and simultaneously in Canada
by Random House of Canada Limited, Toronto.

Library of Congress Cataloging in Publication Data:
Estes, Rose.
    Children of the dragon.
    SUMMARY: In the mythical kingdom of Gallardia, the Dragon-
lord's three children must fight to save themselves and the one
remaining egg of the guardian dragon.
    1. Children's stories, American.   [1. Dragons—Fiction.
2. Fantasy]   I. Lundgren, Carl, ill.   II. Title.
PZ7.E7496Ch   1985   [Fic]   84-22318
ISBN: 0-394-86433-6 (pbk.); 0-394-96433-0 (lib. bdg.)

Manufactured in the United States of America
1 2 3 4 5 6 7 8 9 0

This book is dedicated to
Mike Short *and* Madge Moody,
who accompanied me into the darkness
and helped me map the unknown.

Contents

Children of the Dragon

Long ago . . .

and very far away there was once a small kingdom called Gallardia. Gallardia was a beautiful place, a lush green valley sheltered from the worst of weather by the peaks of great mountains which circled it completely.

To the north lay the military kingdom of Bilbergia, always ready to attack a neighbor. To the east, the Great Ocean of Mists, traveled only by the Sea Folk, a moody and dangerous people. Vast, hot deserts lay to the south, thinly populated by nomadic herders and strange wild animals. To the west were the unknown lands, a place of mystery which few people entered and from which no one ever returned.

Gallardia was a peaceful country of farmers, artisans and merchants. It was ruled from a modest palace by a timid king who seldom bothered anyone. The people lived in small rural villages, the largest of which was also named Gallardia.

The valley had been settled many lifetimes earlier by people fleeing the tyranny and chaos of the lands beyond. No one knew for certain how those first people had come into the country. Entrance to the valley was through a high mountain pass, and it was guarded by a fierce green dragon named Tecla.

Somehow a bargain was struck with the dragon, and the settlers occupied the valley with Tecla as their protector. In return, they provided her (for the dragon was a female) with food and gold.

The exchange worked well for generations, benefiting both people and dragon. The dragon was tended by a hereditary Dragonlord (who was really more important than the king), and over the long years she grew fat and wealthy. Undisturbed by war, the people prospered—and slowly forgot that they had the dragon to thank.

And then, quite unexpectedly, the aging dragon laid a clutch of eggs, and nothing was ever the same again.

1

Leaving Home

"I don't want to live in the cave with the dragon," Lydia said sullenly. "I bet it's cold and damp and full of spiders. Why do we have to go? Nobody in Gallardia would hurt us. The people are our friends."

"I'd like to believe that," replied her father. "But I can't take a chance. People might strike first and remember friendship later. If moving to the cave will keep you and your brothers safe, then we must go."

"But why are the villagers mad at us? It's not our fault the dragon laid eggs!"

"Because I am the Dragonlord," said Godwin. "I am the one who collects their cattle and chickens to feed the dragon. I am the one who gathers the gold she requires for protecting the valley. People fear that once the eggs hatch, their Dragon Dues will increase. And since they dare not oppose the dragon, they will take their anger out on us."

"It's not fair!" said Lydia. "The dragon's so old. Why didn't she just die instead of having all those stupid eggs? Then we could have been normal like everyone else!"

"Come here, pumpkin," Godwin said patiently to the tall, lean child whose darkly tanned face was flushed with anger. Seating himself in the old rocker where his wife had once rocked their children, he drew his daughter onto his knee.

"You're eleven now, sweetheart," he said as he stroked her long blond hair. "That's old enough to understand that sometimes you have to do things you don't like. This is hard on all of us, even me. It would help a lot if you tried to understand."

He smoothed the angry frown from her face with the tip of a finger and traced the straight brown brows and slender nose. As he tickled the stubborn little chin he was rewarded with a reluctant smile and the hint of a dimple.

"If you keep frowning like that you'll scare all the boys away," he teased.

"Oh, Father, boys are dumb. I don't care about them," she said, but the tension eased from her body and she snuggled against his broad chest.

Godwin rocked his unhappy daughter and gathered strength from the large friendly room that had been his home for so long.

"I know it's been difficult for you since your mother died," he said softly. "I have to be away so often collecting the Dragon Dues, and Granny Roone is getting old, but you must know that I love you very, very much."

"I know, Father," said Lydia as she buried her face in the hollow of his neck, "but sometimes I wish you were a farmer instead of a Dragonlord."

"There have been times when I too wished to be something else," admitted Godwin, "but I never had a choice. My father was Dragonlord and his father before him and his father before him. It was my birthright and my duty, as it will one day be your brother's."

Lydia said with a sniff, "I'd be better at it than Daniel."

"Chickens can't be peacocks, no matter how hard they try, and girls can't be Dragonlords," said Godwin. "You mustn't try to be something you're not. Be content with being a girl."

"Oh, Father, you don't understand

anything!" cried Lydia, her brown eyes snapping with anger. Leaping to her feet, she ran to her room and slammed the door behind her.

Godwin sighed deeply. Settling in the rocker, he looked around as though fixing the room in his memory. Soft rag rugs woven by Granny Roone, the children's nurse, covered the flagstone floor, and picture books stood next to plates on the shelves. Fuzzy kittens slept on the warm hearth where cinnamon buns browned slowly. Broad beams of sunlight streaked through the window, turning the geraniums on the broad sills a glowing red. A stab of grief twisted Godwin's heart. He whispered a prayer, fearing that he might never see this beloved room again.

Shaking the thought from him, he crossed to the door and called his sons. Raucous cries echoed from a nearby wood and soon the two boys were racing toward him.

His older son, Daniel, a tall gangling youth of thirteen, straightened with a laugh, running his fingers through the rumpled blond hair that framed his oval face. His eyes were green, and his nose was straight and slender with a light dusting of freckles. Gazing fondly at the boy, Godwin prayed he would have time to prepare him for the responsibilities of being Dragonlord.

A smile tugged at his lips as he looked at

his younger son. Barely seven summers, Max was like a small brown puppy. He had a little round face with a pointy chin. A mop of thick brown hair hung over his bright hazel eyes, barely concealing a pair of very large ears.

There were so many differences in his children, thought Godwin. Daniel was slow and cautious in both thought and deed while Lydia was quick and sharp. Daniel seemed happiest roaming the forest. But Max and Lydia were seldom alone, preferring the company of others.

"Gather your things, boys," said Godwin. "We're going to be spending some time at the cave."

"Hooray!" cried Max. "Can I sleep in the nest with the eggs?"

"No, you silly," Daniel chided him gently. "I know Tecla likes you, but she won't let you near the nest. I tried it last week and she singed the ground near my feet."

"She will too let me," Max said defiantly. "She's my best friend."

"We'll see," said Godwin. "Right now I want you to gather clothes for a week, your books and one favorite thing."

"I'll take a book," said Daniel.

"And I'll take the kittens," said Max.

"No kittens," Godwin said firmly. "They're too little to leave their mother and they'll be here when we get back. Take something else, preferably not alive."

As the boys left to do their father's bidding, Godwin unlocked the corner cabinet and took a knife and a sword from its depths.

"Must you do this, sir?" asked a tearful voice. Turning, Godwin saw the aproned bulk of Granny Roone filling the outer doorway.

"Don't cry, Granny," said Godwin as he hugged the faithful nurse. "We'll only be gone a few days."

"I know," sobbed Granny. "But why do you have to take my babies? Surely they'll be safer here if there's trouble."

"Nothing's going to happen, Granny. People will come to their senses and settle down soon. But until they do, it'll be safer for us at the cave."

"Then I'm coming too!" cried Granny. "I've looked after those children since they were born. They need me and you don't know the first thing about taking care of them. Why, you'll probably all starve up there in that cave!"

"Granny, you're not coming with us," Godwin said gently. "It's cold up there and your bones would ache. We'll be fine, I promise. But if you want to do something to help, why not get the children ready and then pack some food for us?"

Honking into her handkerchief, Granny tugged at her cap and straightened her apron.

"Mind you, Godwin, I'll never forgive you if you get yourself killed. I know you didn't start this trouble, but that dragon has been taking care of herself for a long time. If the fools do start something, let the dragon do her own fighting. You and the children mean more to me than my own family. I couldn't stand it if anything happened to you."

"Don't worry, Granny, nothing's going to happen to us. I give you my word. Now, enough of this talk. Off with you! See to the children and we'll be back before you know it!"

They left the next morning, with Granny in the doorway waving good-bye.

"I don't see why we have to leave so early," grumbled Lydia as the horses clopped quietly down the misty cobblestone streets. "Everyone's still asleep."

"That's the whole point," answered Godwin. "Our presence is a constant reminder of the dragon. If people don't see us, they might calm down long enough for me to reason with them."

"I don't think so," said Lydia. "Vanda says that her uncle Iestyn hates you. He's telling everyone that you're going to turn the

11

dragons into an army and then everyone in the valley will have to do what you say!"

"Lydia!" Daniel gasped in horror. "You know that Father would never do that! You mustn't say such things!"

"Oh, Daniel!" Lydia cried in exasperation. "I never said Father would do that. Vanda did. I can't help it if her uncle is jealous of Father. Even you have to admit that Iestyn hates Father and would do anything to hurt him."

As she spoke Iestyn's blacksmith shop rose out of the morning mists and even Lydia fell silent as they rode past the dilapidated building. The dirty windows showed no light and the doors sagged tight against the lock, yet it seemed as though something cold and evil watched them till they were out of sight.

Familiar landmarks appeared briefly in the mist—the bakery, the toy shop, Vanda's house, the guard post, the simple two-story palace of the king with a sleeping guard in front, the elaborate stone-carved Temple of the Gods. A heavy sadness filled the family as they left the village.

Wrapped in their thoughts, they rode silently through the lush green fields of spring. Cattle drowsed in the thin, early light and the thick grass sighed gently in the breeze.

Swathed in a warm blue cloak, little Max fell behind the others and looked back at the sleeping town. "Good-bye, kittens. Good-bye, town. Good-bye, Granny," he whispered. "I'll be back soon. I pray you don't forget me."

Then, turning toward the snow-capped mountains to the north, he rode to join his family.

2

The Evil Plan

Iestyn stood at the grimy window of his workshop and watched Godwin and his family ride by. A bitter smile crossed his dark face.

"It will not help you to flee," he whispered. "I know where you're going. The dragon cannot protect you, she is old and close to death. And when she dies, everything will be mine.

"I have not forgotten, Godwin. I remember everything, from the first fight when we were boys, to Janet's death. If she'd married me, she'd be alive today. But she married you and died bearing your brats. You will pay, and the price will be high."

"Iestyn, what are you doing in here at this hour?" called a woman's voice from the door that connected the forge to the barn beyond. "It's cold and there's no fire."

Iestyn turned from the window and faced his wife, a tall, plain woman who had never understood his yearnings.

"Leave me to my thoughts, Sarah."

"Thoughts are better if they are shared, husband. Come back to bed."

"Leave me alone!" said Iestyn, and turning to the glass, he watched Godwin ride out of town.

"Godwin again," murmured the woman as she moved to her husband's side. "Iestyn, give up this senseless jealousy," she said, placing her hand on his muscular arm. "This hatred is changing you into a man I scarcely know. Where is the good, kind man I married? Leave Godwin and his children to themselves. You have a son and a wife of your own."

"You don't understand, Sarah," said Iestyn, groaning. His black eyes blinked with pain. Hatred was consuming him. It ate at him every moment of every day and whispered in his ear when he slept. "All my life Godwin has taken from me! And now those cursed dragon eggs of his will hatch and we will be burdened with more taxes. I say it is enough. There must be an end to it! And everyone agrees with me."

"No, Iestyn," said the woman as she

pulled her shawl around her thin shoulders. "Most people are worried about the dragon eggs, but they trust Godwin to find a solution. The only people who agree with you are the scum you drink with down at the Dragon's Breath. You wouldn't have given that rabble the time of day a year ago. Why are you doing so now?"

Iestyn's craggy face closed to his wife's questioning gaze.

"Give up this madness, Iestyn," begged the woman. "I know you're plotting something evil. I can feel it. It flows from you like heat. I beg you to stop."

"So he's fooled you, too," Iestyn said bitterly. "My own wife. I should have known. Leave me alone, Sarah. There is nothing more to say."

"Iestyn!" cried the woman, and she put her hand on his shoulder. But he turned his back to her and stood like stone. At last she crept away to their house next door and left him to his lonely thoughts.

All day Iestyn worked at his forge, pumping the bellows till the coals glowed white with heat, pounding the metal till it bent beneath the blows of his short, muscular body.

As night fell thunder began to roll and great sheets of rain drove against the flimsy windows. Casting off his leather apron,

Iestyn wrapped himself against the storm and stalked down the rainswept street to the sign of the Dragon's Breath. Throngs of men were crowded around the wooden tables within. Iestyn took his mug from its peg on the wall and filled it with ale from a large keg. Then, closing his ears to the welcoming calls of fellow craftsmen, he pushed his way to the back of the long, oak-paneled room and sat alone in the darkest corner.

As the evening advanced he was joined by a number of men who slunk through the doorway one by one, filled their mugs and gathered round his table. The look of them kept others at a distance.

"Well, what's the plan, mate?" asked a brawny fellow with one eye. "None of us want to be seen here, all in public, together, if you gets my meaning."

"What I have to say will make it worth your while, Wulf," said Iestyn. "I'm going to make you rich."

The men fell silent at the mention of money. Every squinty, beady, greedy eye fastened on the blacksmith.

"I speak of the dragon," said Iestyn. At his words, curses were uttered and the men slumped in disgust.

"Look, Iestyn, give it up," said a thin man named Quinby as he spat a stream of tobacco juice. "We've all heard your complaints about the Dragonlord. You know we can't touch him. To harm him or his family is a King's Offense and I've no wish to swing on the gallows to satisfy your quarrel."

As the man started to rise Iestyn said, "Enough gold to make each of you a king, and no one to know."

Wulf blinked his one good eye and sat down. "Speak," he said.

"The dragon is old, and soon she will die," said Iestyn.

"What does it matter?" said a small man named Weylin, who was cleaning his nails with the tip of a razor-sharp knife. "Soon there will be more dragons to take her place, and tenfold more in taxes."

"Not if we take the eggs," said Iestyn.

"Take the eggs!" squeaked a weak-chinned fellow named Arbus. "The dragon will kill us!"

"Not so," Iestyn said calmly as he took a drink of ale. "Tomorrow it is my turn to provide the Dragon Dues—two fat cows, twenty hens and four gold pieces. I could dose the creatures with a potion of my own making. By the second dawn the dragon would be dead, and we could take the eggs and enough gold to keep each of us for a life-time."

"Kill the dragon?" whispered a man

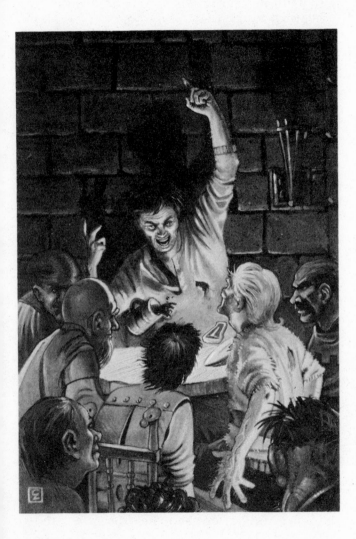

named Malac. All sat silent, testing the awful thought in their minds.

"Well, she *is* going to die soon," said Quinby. "It would sort of be a mercy, putting her out of her misery a bit early so she don't suffer none."

"But—but, you can't kill the dragon," whispered Arbus, his chin all but disappearing as he hung his head. "It would be wrong. It would hurt her and—and I like her. I've changed my mind. Do this without me." He stumbled to his feet, knocking over his chair.

As he hurried away, the little man with the knife rose swiftly and followed him out the door.

The men sat, each avoiding the others' eyes until Weylin returned, rain streaming from his clothes. He nodded once, and after a moment the talk continued.

"Dragon eggs are rare and seldom seen," Iestyn said softly. "There are many who would pay for such a thing."

"Bilbergia would offer a great deal," muttered a nasty-looking fellow named Kray.

"As would the desert people," added Wulf.

"I think the Sea Folk would take several," said a large, broad-chested man named Ulpha as he cracked his knuckles and grinned.

"Don't forget the caravans," added Quinby. "They travel far and wide and could sell the eggs to those who know nothing of us."

"It will not matter what they know, for we will not be here," said Iestyn.

"Leave Gallardia?" rumbled Ulpha.

"Far behind us," Iestyn said with a smile. "Why stay here when we can go anywhere in the world?"

"I won't be unhappy to leave," said Weylin. "But I'll settle some accounts before I go."

"Do what you will," said Iestyn, "but meet me here in two nights with weapons and a straw-filled wagon, ready to travel."

"Weapons?" asked the last of the conspirators, a man named Olwen. "Why do we need weapons? If the dragon is dead, all we need do is load the eggs and drive away."

"It never hurts to be prepared," said Iestyn as he bent to his mug.

"And what of your old foe, the Dragonlord?" asked Weylin. "Where will he be during all this? He's not going to let us take the eggs without a fight."

"The Dragonlord and his family have left on a trip to collect dues in the south," Iestyn lied smoothly. "I saw them leave myself. The old woman says they'll be gone for a fortnight. By the time they return, the deed will be done. It will be thought that the dragon died of natural causes and none will cry foul play."

"But what of the eggs? The game will be up as soon as they're found to be gone."

"We will break one and make it seem as though wild animals stole and ate the rest," answered Iestyn.

"Break an egg!" gasped Olwen. "We can't do that. They're worth a fortune!"

"Don't be a fool!" snapped Iestyn. "That dragon's been collecting gold for hundreds and hundreds of years. There's enough wealth in that cave for us to live like kings for ten lifetimes! One egg means nothing! Now stop your tongue! Either you're with me or you're against me!"

Some few hesitated. Then, glancing sidelong at Weylin and his knife, each added his aye, till there were none who said no.

"Then we are agreed," said Iestyn. "Let us shake on it to seal the bargain." And one by one, each of the men placed his hand atop the hand of another, till all were piled high.

"It is done," Iestyn said with satisfaction. "Let no one speak of this on pain of death!"

"Death," echoed the men, and then each in his turn left the table and crept out into the wet night.

3

In the Dragon's Cave

The dragon's cave was located far to the north, high in the single pass through the mountains that surrounded Gallardia. The journey there took Godwin and his family nearly a full day. Shortly before sundown they turned their exhausted horses out into a tiny mountain pasture. Then, slinging their bundles over their shoulders, they walked the final distance to the dragon's lair.

As they entered the narrow pass there was a tremendous roar, and a blast of hot air plastered their clothes against their bodies. Lydia looked about nervously as small pebbles rained down from the granite cliffs that rose steeply on either side.

"Don't worry, pumpkin," said Godwin,

squeezing her shoulder. "Tecla knows it's us; she's just teasing."

"H-how can you be sure?" said Lydia, trying to bring her shaking voice under control.

"Because she recognizes my footstep," said Godwin, "and probably Daniel's and Max's as well. See these scorch marks?" He pointed to dark lines that stained the cliffs. "That happened when I was a boy. A party of bandits tried to slip past her while she slept. Tecla flamed them to crisps; even their swords were melted. She has very sensitive hearing. No one could possibly get through the pass without being heard."

Lydia shrugged and tossed her hair back over her shoulder. "I wasn't really afraid," she said haughtily. "I was just surprised."

Hiding a smile, Godwin ushered his children forward against the gusting winds.

The wind struck them like a blow as they turned the final bend, for while the mountain continued climbing on their left it fell away steeply on their right, leaving only the narrow ribbon of road before plunging to the abyss below.

An eagle screamed in the cold, thin air and drifted by on outstretched wings. Max reached for his father's hand. "This part always scares me," he confided in a small voice.

"You *should* be scared," said Godwin, gripping the little hand tightly. "It's a dangerous place. Grown men have been swept to their deaths by these winds. The pass would be dangerous even without the dragon."

Drawing their cloaks around them and holding their bundles tightly, the small group hugged the cliff and edged their way toward the large cave that lay ahead, opening into the side of the mountain.

Suddenly a huge green scaly head, topped by a fringed crest, thrust itself out of the cave and stared at them. The creature peered closely at Lydia, who stood very, very still. Gold eyes glinted and a forked tongue tasted the air. Then, just as suddenly as she had appeared, the dragon withdrew.

Feeling small and edible, Lydia entered the cave for the first time. For a moment all was darkness. Then, as her eyes adjusted to the gloom, she saw the immense dragon, thirty feet long from head to tail, crouched on an even larger nest of sticks and hay. The dragon had built her nest just inside the entrance to the cave, where she could easily survey the pass. Behind the nest, rising in ridges like a small mountain range, lay the vast hoard of dragon gold.

"Put our things over there," Godwin told Lydia, pointing to an alcove on the right-hand wall, opposite the dragon's nest.

One by one, the children dropped their bundles and sagged to the floor.

Over the years each of the Dragonlords had added small comforts to that part of the dragon's cave which they called their own, until it had become a pleasant place to stay while carrying out their duties.

In his own time Godwin had covered the cold stone floor with soft rugs made of wool from his own sheep and dyed, spun and woven by Granny Roone. Large, over-stuffed cushions, also made by the old nurse, provided seating. Torches attached to the wall, and a firepit sunk in the floor, cast light as well as heat. Books, clothes and food were stored on the shelves that had been carved in the cave wall by Godwin's ancestors.

High on the wall, in its own special niche, was a burnished wood statue of Hespus, the family's household god. It was a smaller copy of the one at home. Offerings were made to Hespus in hopes of his protection within the family walls. Outside those walls, the greater Gods had to be invoked. To be safe Godwin often called on the Gods as well as Hespus when he was in the cave, for he was never sure how far Hespus's power extended. The alcove was but a tiny corner of the huge cavern, which rose high above the

Dragonlord's head and continued far into the flank of the mountain.

A deep rumbling now filled the cave and the very walls and floor seemed to tremble.

"I'm coming! I'm coming!" cried Max as he stowed his bundle on his sleep mat and ran joyfully to greet the dragon.

"That's Tecla's way of purring," Daniel said to Lydia. "She has lots of noises, just like a cat. After you're around her for a while, you get to recognize them and what they mean."

"Who cares," Lydia said with a sniff. She stood up and placed her one souvenir of home, a little carved wooden horse, in the niche with the household god. "I don't even like dragons," she added.

"Lydia! Don't say that!" Daniel whispered in shock, glancing toward Tecla.

"Oh, Daniel, I was only joking," Lydia said in disgust. "But I've never even been here before. If Father would bring me up here as often as he brings you, I'd understand her too. And probably better than you do."

"Lydia, it's not a contest," said Daniel in the calm, patronizing voice that always annoyed her. "Besides, there's no reason for you to learn about Tecla. I'm the one who's going to be Dragonlord. You're a girl, all you have to do is grow up and get married."

"Oh, you make me so mad!" cried Lydia. "Neither you nor Father understands a thing!" To her horror, she felt angry tears spring to her eyes.

It's not fair, thought Lydia as she turned away blindly, dashing the tears from her face. They never ask me what I'd like to do, it's always "Stay at home, Lydia." "Try to be more ladylike, Lydia." "Oh, no, you can't cut your hair, Lydia, it's much too pretty long." What right do they have to plan my life for me? I have a few plans of my own and they don't include marrying some dumb boy!

"Don't worry, Daniel," said Godwin as they watched her stamp away angrily. "She was mad at *me* yesterday. Let her alone for a little while and she'll forget it by dinnertime."

"I'm just glad she's not a boy," Daniel said ruefully. "She's got an awful temper, and she can punch hard too."

The dim light in the cave was kind to the dragon, hiding the missing scales and the withered wings. It was easy to imagine her as she must have been in her fiery youth. As Lydia drew closer to the great creature, her heart thumped unevenly and she was afraid. In spite of her angry words, she was very glad when her father joined her and slipped his hand into hers.

Together they approached the great beast as she sat high atop her nest. Max peered over the edge of the nest and grinned at them. As he had predicted, the dragon had not minded when he scrambled up to join her.

Godwin reached up and stroked Tecla's massive head as it came to rest lightly on his shoulder, and the dragon's rumbling took on a deeper, throatier tone.

"Glad to see me, old girl?" Godwin murmured quietly. "How's the family? Are we going to see them soon?"

"Does she understand you, Father?" asked Lydia.

"When she wants to," said Godwin. "But if what I say is not to her liking, she ignores me."

The dragon exhaled softly, and to Lydia it sounded like laughter.

"I have heard that there are those who can actually speak with dragons," Godwin said wistfully.

"Then why can't you?" asked Lydia.

"I've tried," said Godwin. "But it's a gift I do not have."

"You could learn," persisted Lydia.

"Ah, we're too old, she and I," said Godwin. "It's too late for us. But it's said that when a dragon is born, sometimes it will bond with a human, and then the two are linked for life. This is another reason we are here. By all signs the egg will hatch soon, and when they do I want Daniel close. It's my hope that he will form such a bond with one of the dragons. With such a power, a man could go far in this world."

Or a woman, thought Lydia as she stared into the huge gold eye. So could a woman.

4

The Tale of the Dragon

Night had fallen and the cold north wind howled through the pass. Rain beat down heavily. Inside the cave, Godwin's campfire reflected off the mountains of dragon gold and bathed the room in pale, warm light.

The dragon had been groomed with soft silk clothes and soothed to sleep. Gentle, steamy snores rumbled from her great nostrils, filling the air with warmth as she lay curled around her unborn brood.

Their duties done and supper bubbling on the fire, the Dragonlord and his family relaxed in the alcove. For the first time in weeks, Godwin enjoyed the luxurious feeling of safety.

"Now, pumpkin," Godwin said with a twinkle in his eye. "About those spiders—"

"Well, I didn't know there weren't any," said Lydia. "You never bring me here."

"A woman's place is in the home," said Godwin. "There's never been a reason for you to come before now."

Hot words sprang to Lydia's lips but before she could speak, Max leaned against his father's knee and said, "Let's not fight. Tell us the story, Father."

"Oh, Max, we've heard it a million times," said Daniel. "Father doesn't want to tell it again."

"I don't mind," said Godwin as he stroked Max's silky brown hair. "It's an important tale and one that should be told often, to keep us from forgetting."

Lighting his pipe with a twig from the fire, Godwin gazed into the flames and began:

"Long ago, farther back than memory goes, the dragon lived in Gallardia. It was her home and she roamed the skies freely. Then one day people appeared; it is said they were fleeing an evil king in the north. No records remain of them, who they were or how they escaped the dragon, but somehow they entered the valley. Soon they had conquered it, turning its rich soil to their plows and taming the wild cattle and horses for their use. They worked hard, formed a government and did well, or would have, had it not been for the dragon."

"Why?" asked Max, who knew the story by heart.

"Because she would swoop down out of the sky as fast as lightning, wings spread wide and breathing fire, and snatch up a fatted cow, or even worse, a person."

"And what happened then?" prompted Daniel.

"Well, Farbus the First, who was king at that time, left a letter for the dragon, begging her not to eat his people."

"That was dumb," said Lydia with a snort. "Dragons can't read!"

"Quite true," said Godwin, "and the devastation continued."

"What did the king do then?" asked Max.

"He sent out a messenger," answered Godwin, "a man who had broken many of the new laws, to deliver the message in person. Farbus promised that if he delivered the message and returned, he would be pardoned of his crimes. Unfortunately he did not return.

"Farbus used this method to rid his tiny kingdom of troublemakers—and irritating relatives—for a number of years. Then, to his amazement, one of the messengers actually returned! It seems that over the years the dragon had received bits and pieces of the message until at last she had digested the whole thing. She signaled her approval of the plan by returning the messenger alive."

"But she ate his horse!" Max added with a giggle.

"And that's when the Dragonlords first began," said Daniel.

"Right," said Godwin. "Farbus created the position of Dragonlord and set the plan in action. As you know, your great-great-great-great-grandfather was the very first Dragonlord, and thereafter, every first-born son took the title upon his father's death."

"And that's when the Dragon Dues started," said Lydia.

"Right," said Godwin. "For that was Farbus's bargain. Each family was to pay a portion of their wealth to the dragon in the form of gold, cattle and other livestock. In return the dragon was to cease raiding the valley and protect it from its enemies.

"It was a good plan, and it worked to the advantage of all," said Godwin, "for the dragon grew fat and rich and the people lived without fear."

"If it worked so well, how come everyone hates Dragon Dues now?" asked Lydia.

"The dragon did her job too well," said Godwin with a sigh as he tapped his pipe into the fire. "Our enemies learned quickly and no one has tried to invade Gallardia for a long time."

"Well, what's wrong with that?" asked Lydia.

"The people feel safe," said Godwin. "They don't think the dragon is necessary anymore and they resent paying her with their hard-earned gold and cattle."

"But if there were no dragon and Bilbergia attacked us, what would we do?" asked Daniel.

"We'd lose," answered Godwin. "But no one seems to realize that except us."

"What about the king, old Farbus the Fat?" cried Lydia. "Why doesn't he say something!"

"Hold your tongue, child," said Godwin. "He's still the king and I'll not have you speak of him with disrespect."

"But Father, Lydia's right," Daniel argued calmly. "Why doesn't the king say something to the people? After all, it was his ancestor who made the original bargain and created the Dragon Dues. They're not your doing and it's wrong for the people to be angry with you."

"He's not a very brave king," said Godwin, "and I suppose he resents the dues as much as any other man, since he must pay even more than most."

"But he should pay more!" cried Max. "He's richer than anyone else!"

"True," said Godwin, "but that doesn't mean he has to like paying his dues. And I suppose that since he provides me with a house and land and a yearly salary, he considers that being disliked is part of my job."

"That's not fair," said Daniel.

"Little in life is," answered Godwin.

"Lots of people think the dragon is too old to defend us, even if we needed her," said Lydia. "They say she's lost her fire."

"I wish you could have seen her before," said Godwin, looking back over the years. "When I was young, her scales were as hard as metal and sparkled like fire. When she flew, she mirrored the sun and it hurt your eyes to look at her. She could stay aloft for days at a time. With her wings spread wide to catch the currents, she was a sight to behold."

"I bet she was beautiful," Daniel said sadly.

"She was indeed," said Godwin with a smile. "And she still is, to me."

"Why aren't there more dragons?" asked Lydia.

"I don't know," answered Godwin. "I don't think there were ever very many and I suspect they have fared badly in their battles with man."

"But how can that be?" asked Daniel. "Dragons are so big and men are so small."

"Yes, but there are many more men than there are dragons. If all dragons eat as much as ours does, then I know people would find a way to kill them."

"That's horrible!" cried Lydia. "You can't just kill something because it eats your cow!"

"Unfortunately others don't share your views," Godwin said in a low voice. "I've just learned that the Sea Folk have slain the black dragon of the Steaming Straits."

No sooner had he spoken than there was an anguished roar, and a spurt of fire flashed out of the dragon's mouth and flared through the cavern.

As Lydia screamed and the boys scrambled behind their father, the dragon lurched out of her nest. Throwing back her head, she roared again and again, till it seemed that the cave must collapse around her.

Godwin cursed his careless words and the dragon's sensitive hearing as he recalled the rumors of Tecla's mating with the black dragon. Hand outstretched, he approached her, speaking gently but clearly. His voice cut through the stricken bellows.

"Hush, Tecla, calm yourself. My words were thoughtless and I do not know them to be true. It could be that the Sea Folk lied as they often do and this dragon still sails the skies.

"Come, lie back down, my sweet. Think of the eggs; you must keep them warm."

Slowly, slowly, Godwin's words calmed the anguished beast and the madness ebbed away. Drooping weakly, the dragon returned to her nest and curled herself upon her eggs.

"Will she be all right, Father?" asked Daniel.

"I think so, son," said Godwin as he stood next to the nest and stroked the long slender neck. "But we must let her know that we care and that we will not let any harm come to her."

Waving the children back to the campfire, Godwin stayed with the dragon. The last thing the children heard as they drifted into sleep was his words of comfort and love.

5

An Angry Meeting

Iestyn watched with satisfaction as the two cows and twenty hens in his barn ate the grain he had prepared. Then he counted out four heavy gold pieces and placed them in a small leather pouch. Usually the blacksmith resented having to deliver his Dragon Dues to the dragon's mountain himself, as was the custom for people living in the north of Gallardia. But today the custom suited his schemes.

A broad smile creased his rugged face. Pulling a cap over his coarse black hair, he began to whistle.

"Good morning, Father," called a voice.

"Why, good morning to you, Godfrey," Iestyn said cheerfully as he turned and saw his son, a boy of fifteen, standing in the doorway of the barn. Already taller than his father, Godfrey was as fair as his father was dark. His young face had a look of strength about it, in the direct blue eyes and the strong square chin. Dressed crudely but neatly in rough brown homespun shirt and pants, Godfrey studied his father's smile and wondered at the cause of this unexpected good humor.

"Is something wrong, Father?" he asked cautiously.

"Wrong? What could possibly be wrong?" asked Iestyn with a broad smile. "As a matter of fact, everything will soon be right!"

"You're taking the cattle up the mountain today, aren't you, Father? May I come with you? You'll need someone to help."

Iestyn's thick black brows lowered and his smile turned to a frown. "And I don't suppose you'd mind if we just happened to run into that little snippet Lydia, would you?"

A bright flush covered Godfrey's cheeks. Brushing his hair back from his face, he met his father's eyes squarely and said, "Lydia, Daniel and little Max are my friends. I don't understand why you dislike them so much. They've never done anything to you."

"They haven't, eh?" said Iestyn, taking a threatening step toward his son, who quickly stepped back. "I have my reasons," the blacksmith said coldly, "but I don't have to explain them to you or to anyone else!"

"All right, Father," Godfrey said carefully. Then, after a moment's pause, he asked, "May I come?"

"You can come if you wish," Iestyn answered roughly, "but see to it that you stay out of my way."

Before long father and son were off, the chickens in crates and the cows tied to the back of the horse-drawn wagon, following quietly behind.

As the sun's rays burned away the morning mist, Godfrey asked, "Father, why are the animals so quiet? Are they sick?"

"Of course not," Iestyn said quickly. "I just gave them something to calm them. It will help them go to their fate more easily."

Godfrey looked at his father, amazed. Iestyn stared back, daring the boy to speak.

"Why so surprised, boy?" he said. "I've raised these creatures since they were born. It's bad enough to see them go for dragon fodder. I've no wish for them to suffer."

Godfrey looked at the grim, dark man who was his father and wondered at his sudden, swift shifts of mood. "I'm glad you did it," he said.

A small smile crossed Iestyn's face. "Yes. I'm glad too," he replied.

The day passed without incident. Their progress was slow but steady, although they stopped several times when the cattle stumbled and faltered.

"Perhaps I made the potion too strong," said Iestyn. "But don't worry, everything will be all right in the end."

Urging the cattle along, they arrived near dark at the animal pens which lay well up on the mountainside, several miles from the dragon's lair. Iestyn put the sluggish cows into one pen while Godfrey emptied the chicken crates into another. For once the hens did not squawk and flutter as they gained their freedom, but settled quietly to the ground.

Daniel and Godwin arrived on horseback just as Iestyn closed the heavy wood bars on the circular cattle pen. Godfrey smiled at Daniel but knew better than to speak.

"Well, Dragonlord," said Iestyn, leaning against the rough wood gate, "here are your Dragon Dues, and may she choke on them."

"She is not my dragon, Iestyn," Godwin said calmly as he and Daniel dismounted. "She belongs to the people."

"Ha!" said Iestyn. "If that were true, I would give her away. She's too expensive for a pet, and she eats too much."

"She has earned her keep many times over," replied Godwin. "We would have been Bilbergian slaves long ago if not for her."

"So you say, Dragonlord. I think we could take care of ourselves. But that's not the quarrel now, one single dragon. What are we to do with all those soon to hatch? Other than increase our offerings? Soon we will all be paupers, working only to feed a gaggle of flying lizards!"

"We must wait and see what happens," Godwin answered carefully. "It may be that, as with chickens, some of the eggs will not hatch. First we must see how many dragonlings there are. Then, calmly and in Council, we may all decide what to do. And if the dragon dies, as now seems likely, we will need a new dragon to take her place."

"What if all the eggs survive and the old dragon lives?" snarled Iestyn. "Then what, Dragonman? Then you would have an army to do your bidding. No man could defy you. Gallardia, Bilbergia and all the world beyond would be yours to command.

"You think you have everyone fooled. Well, you don't fool me, Lizardman! I see through your plan. You want to take over. But I'm not going to let you. I'm going to stop you and your brats. Your reign is finished. Believe it!"

The two men glared at each other, one small, dark and muscular, the other tall, fair and finely built. Iestyn twitched with tension and his hand edged toward his dagger. The two boys watched their fathers in shock.

"Iestyn, this quarrel is between us and has nothing to do with dragons or children," said Godwin, controlling his anger with effort. "Do not make threats against those who are blameless. Let us strike a truce—"

Iestyn barked a short, harsh laugh.

"And after the eggs are hatched," continued Godwin, "you and I will take your quarrel to the Settlement Grounds and finish the matter there, with swords, once and for all!"

Daniel cried out, and Godfrey stood frozen by the wagon.

"You'd like that, wouldn't you!" snarled Iestyn. "With your height and longer reach!"

"Damn you, man! What would you have me do!" Godwin cried in exasperation.

"Die," said Iestyn. "Die. Only then will I be satisfied."

"You're mad!" said Godwin, a pulse beating strongly at his temple. "I've never harmed you. You're imagining these wrongs. They spring from your own twisted mind. Think what you like, but don't blame me for your own shortcomings!"

Godwin's horse threw up its head and pranced nervously behind him.

"I don't intend to die, Iestyn," the

Dragonlord continued. "Nor will I let you harm anyone under my care. Stay away from my children and the dragons. For if anything happens to them, anything at all, I will hold you to blame!"

"You don't frighten me," spat Iestyn. His face grew dark with rage as he clutched his dagger and took a step forward. "Nor do you command me!"

"No, I don't command you," replied Godwin. "But if you won't settle this with words or swords, then I can only regard you as I would a mad dog running wild."

"Do what you will," sneered Iestyn. "It will not be enough!"

Dipping his hand into his pouch, the blacksmith scooped up the four gold pieces he owed the dragon and flung them at Godwin's feet. Then with a single leap he gained his wagon. As his son scrambled into the back, Iestyn lashed his team cruelly, turned the wagon around and clattered down the mountain. Godwin stared back at them with wide, helpless eyes. The wagon jounced round a bend in the road and was gone.

"Father," said Daniel in a small, frightened voice. "What will he do? What's going to happen?"

"I don't know, son," said Godwin with a sigh. "Probably nothing. His hatred has warped him and he doesn't think clearly, but

I don't believe he'll do anything more than talk."

"But Father, he sounded so angry. How can you be sure? He threatened to kill you! Maybe we should stand guard at night."

"There's nothing to worry about so long as we're with the dragon," said Godwin. "No one can even enter the pass when Tecla's on guard. I'll wager that when we return to the valley, Iestyn will have come to his senses."

"But Father, aren't you scared?"

"Put it from you, Daniel," Godwin said sternly. He gripped his son's shoulders and looked into his eyes. "Fear serves only the enemy. It defeats you before the battle is ever fought. I'm not frightened of Iestyn. I respect his hatred and that serves me better than fear. I do not wish to fight him, but if I must, I will.

"Now come, we must leave. Tecla is waiting to fly down for her dinner. I can almost hear her stomach rumbling. And mind you, not a word of this to the others. There's no reason to upset them."

Daniel gathered the four coins for his father, and together they rode up into the pass toward the hungry dragon.

6

Hopes
and
Fears

As the dragon fed in the pens far below, Godwin led his children over to the great nest.

Constructed of small saplings and sweet hay gathered from the valley, it rose higher than Max's head. Godwin lifted Max onto the edge of the nest and then hoisted Lydia up so she could cling to the lip. Daniel could see into the nest with ease.

"Take a good look, children," said Godwin. "This is a sight few men have seen and lived to talk about."

"Or women," Lydia added under her breath, but she too looked into the nest with awe.

There were ten eggs in the nest. The largest was solid black and towered over its

companions. It was the size of a large water-melon and its shell seemed to glow with a deep intensity, more like a rare gem than a mere eggshell.

The others were a plain dull brown in color and none was half the size of the black egg.

"What is that?" asked Lydia, pointing to a silvery-gray substance that covered the bottom of the nest, cushioning the eggs against sharp edges.

"Castoff dragonskins," answered Godwin. "Every year I help Tecla shed her old skin; then she gathers it up and stores it in the back of the cave. Now I know why. What better cushion for dragon eggs to rest on than dragonskin?

"This is a good-sized clutch," Godwin went on, smiling proudly. "I'd be willing to bet the black egg will be the strongest of the batch, the new leader. The others, if they hatch, will be followers."

"What about that egg, Father?" said Max, pointing into a far corner of the nest.

"Which egg?" asked Godwin. "That big brown one?"

"No, Father. The blue one. It's under the others. Don't you see it?" Max dropped down into the nest to show the egg to his father.

"Why, I hadn't seen it till this moment!"

cried Godwin. "And no wonder, it's almost completely buried by the others. It took your sharp young eyes to see it. Well, let's have a look at it!" And with Daniel and Lydia at his heels, Godwin circled the nest.

Godwin reached into the nest and gently moved a large brown egg to one side, exposing the blue egg that lay beneath. This egg was smaller than all the others and its shell was the pale blue of a robin's egg.

"Oh, Father, it's all lopsided," Lydia said sadly as she touched the tough yet rubbery-feeling shell. "One side is almost flat and the shell is all bumpy. It doesn't look good at all."

"Will it be all right?" asked Daniel. "It's very strange looking."

"I've seen this sort of thing happen with chicken eggs," said Godwin. "If they hatch at all, the chick is almost always deformed. Usually it dies soon after birth. I think we should dispose of this blue egg before it hatches. Tecla has enough to keep her busy."

"You mean kill it?" Max gasped in horror.

"It sounds harsh," said Godwin as he swung Max down to the ground, "but it's really a kindness. I think it would be best."

"You can't do that!" cried Lydia. "It would be murder! And besides, that's just what the villagers want us to do, kill the eggs!"

"Father, what if there's nothing wrong with the egg?" mused Daniel. "What if the shell is just misshapen from the weight of the others? It might be a runt, but they're often feisty and strong. I think we should leave the egg alone and let it take its chances."

"And besides, it's mine. I found it! I won't let you kill it!" Max cried tearfully.

Godwin looked from his younger son, whose eyes brimmed with tears, to the angry, disapproving face of his daughter, to the calm anxious look of his older son.

"Well, it seems as though I'm outnumbered," he said with a smile. "If you feel this strongly, we'll leave the blue egg alone and let fate decide.

"But now it's time to speak of more serious matters. You know I brought you here because our presence in the village was causing problems. But that was not the only reason, though I welcomed it as an excuse for leaving.

"This hatching is an extraordinary event. Very few people in the world know anything about the birth of dragons. Nobody in Gallardia does. What we learn will be of great importance."

"To whom?" asked Daniel. "The way the villagers feel, the dragons won't even get a chance to hatch, much less grow up."

"I'm not worried about the villagers," said

Godwin. "They just talk. And even if they did try something, Tecla would stop them."

"What do you plan to do with the dragon-lings?" asked Lydia.

"I have two plans, actually," said Godwin. "I've been trying to convince Tecla to send them out of the valley to grow up under the protection of other dragons.

"I have also considered sharing them with those few rulers who would use them wisely and for peaceful purposes."

"But Father," said Lydia, "will Tecla agree to either plan?"

"That's the problem." Godwin sighed. "She won't even listen to me. When I try to talk to her about it, she just puts her head under her wing and goes to sleep, or leaves the cave."

"Wouldn't we keep any of them?" asked Max.

"Of course we would," said Godwin. "And that brings me to our main reason for being here. You've heard me speak of dragon hatchings and bondings?"

"I've heard you say it, but I don't understand what it means," said Daniel.

"It's really quite simple," said Godwin. "For example, when ducks or chickens hatch, it's important that they see their mother before they see anything else."

"Why?" asked Max.

"Because they're dumb," answered Lydia. "Whatever they see first they think is their mother and they never change their minds.

"Once, before you were born, Maxie, a fox ate one of our ducks and she had a nest full of eggs. Well, I was there when they hatched and from then on, I had seven honking, squawking baby ducks following me everywhere I went and everyone laughed at me. It was awful!"

"That's not quite what I meant," said Godwin with a smile, "but you've got the general idea. Dragons are a higher form of life than ducks and quite a bit smarter. I don't think they'd confuse you for their mother. But from this moment on, I want one of you children by this nest at all times. At the very first sign that the black egg is hatching, I want Daniel called. And Daniel, make sure you stay near the cave.

"I'm hoping that there's some truth to the old tales. If Daniel is here when the black egg hatches, it's possible that some special bond will be formed between him and the dragonling. It would be the achievement of a lifetime."

"Why the black egg? Why not one of the others?" asked Max. "The blue egg is nice."

"It's very nice, son, but the black egg is the biggest and probably the strongest. I believe it was sired by the black dragon, who was known to be fierce and highly intelligent."

"And dead," Lydia added dryly.

"Possibly," said Godwin with a frown. "If so, then all the more reason for the black egg to live.

"And that brings us to the last reason we are here," Godwin said heavily. "Escape."

"Escape? Why, what do you mean, Father?" Daniel asked in alarm.

"It's quite simple, son," answered Godwin. "One must always be prepared for the worst. I doubt the villagers will attack, but if they do and if the danger grows too great, you children must leave."

"Leave? Leave where?" asked Daniel, a look of fear filling his green eyes.

"Leave here," Godwin answered patiently. "You, Daniel, must wrap the black egg in dragonskin, which is both fireproof and strong, and take it and your sister and brother and leave."

"But what about you?"

"If you have to leave, it will already be too late for me," said Godwin.

Daniel's eyes began to fill with tears and his lower lip trembled.

"Dragonlords do not cry," Godwin said sharply. "I don't expect anything to happen, Daniel, but if it does, you must remember your role in life and do what is required of you. The lives of others rest in your keeping.

"Now, do you remember the old stories about the tunnel under the mountain that Granny Roone used to tell you? Well, they weren't just nursery tales. There is a door to such a tunnel at the back of this cave. My father showed it to me when I was a boy and told me that the tunnel led through the mountain and out the other side. I don't know that for a fact, mind you, for I never traveled it, but my father heard of it from his father, and he from his, and I think the story is true."

"I don't like the dark," said Max with a shaky voice. "I don't want to go there."

"Hush, Max," said Lydia. "We probably won't have to. This is just in case."

"Lydia's right," said Godwin as he knelt beside his son. "But if it becomes necessary, then you must go like a man. I need to know that you won't let me down."

Max's lip quivered as he looked up into his father's eyes. "Do I have to?" he whispered.

"Yes," said Godwin.

"Then I will," said Max, "but I'll still be scared."

"It's all right to be scared," said Godwin. "I probably would be too. Now I'd better show you where the tunnel is before Tecla returns. She's very possessive about her gold and I wouldn't want to test her feelings for us should she find us near it."

Godwin turned and walked into the darker recesses of the cavern, leaving his wide-eyed children to follow.

Their way was quickly blocked by the first great mountain of gold, but Godwin did not slow his pace. Treading on the shimmering wealth as if it were no more than dirt, he staggered up its shifting sides.

The children struggled after him, but no sooner had they reached the top and glimpsed the many mounds that lay beyond, than a cold current of air swept around them.

"Run!" cried Godwin as the breeze blew through the cave. "It's Tecla, she's coming back!"

They slid down the vast pile of gold and raced back to the nest.

"Not a word of this," whispered Godwin, "but don't forget what I have told you."

Seconds later the dragon landed on the ledge outside the cave entrance. Folding her immense wings, she lowered her head and entered the cave. As her eyes adjusted to the dim light, she saw Godwin and his family standing near her unprotected nest, and her fringed crest began to rise, a sure sign of dragon anger.

A soft hiss and a jet of scalding steam

issued from the large fanged mouth as Godwin held up his hand and approached her.

"No need for that, old girl. You know we wouldn't hurt your brood. The children and I were just admiring them. Did you have a good feed?"

7

The Sickness Strikes

The next day passed quickly. Grumbling beneath her breath, Lydia tidied the alcove and prepared the evening meal. Daniel and Godwin rode down to the valley to gather fresh hay for the nest. Max sat at Tecla's feet and sang to her.

Godwin had long ceased trying to keep Max from the dragon. In the earliest days, after his wife's death, he had brought the young child with him when he tended the great beast, unwilling to be separated from the last link with his beloved wife, even for short periods of time.

One day he left the sleeping babe on a woolen fleece in the alcove and set about clearing some fallen rocks from the trail. The task completed, he entered the cave and stopped short. There between the curved claws of the dragon sat the baby. As the huge crested head nuzzled the child, Godwin drew his sword, knowing he could never reach the child in time.

Then the baby laughed and waved its chubby fists, and the great dragon sniffed the small fat body. Godwin froze with fear as the child clutched the dragon's crest and pulled himself to his feet. Max stood there, swaying back and forth on rubbery legs, crowing with excitement and tugging on the delicate fringe. Godwin fully expected to see his son die in a blast of fire. But the dragon did nothing.

One great eye focused on the child and even when the baby sat down with a thump, yanking hard on the crest, the dragon held her breath. The baby bawled and the dragon flicked her forked tongue over his body, turning tears to giggles. And soon, still clutching the fringe, he tried to stand again.

From that day on, Max and the dragon enjoyed a special relationship, one that filled an emptiness, for both were lonely.

Max was deeply loved by his family but sometimes a longing for the mother he had never known filled his heart and he felt separate and alone.

The dragon was alone too. Early in her life the skies had been filled with others of her kind, but as time passed, their numbers dwindled. Females were few and timid and were seldom seen. The males were wild and dangerous and could only be approached at mating time. In truth, the dragon had allowed people into her valley because she was lonely. She observed their actions with interest.

The Dragonlords were a welcome event in her long life, but her huge size, sharp claws and fiery breath kept the men at a distance, so when Godwin's son had crawled toward her that day long ago, she had held her breath and been careful not to move too suddenly. She was rewarded by the tiny creature's trust. Since that day, the two had loved each other with a quiet intensity that not even Godwin realized.

Two years ago the dragon had mated with a small brown dragon above the Western deserts and with a ferocious black male high above the Steaming Straits. On her way home a late storm had blown her off course and into the vast unknown lands that lay west of Gallardia. There, she had met and mated with a beautiful and strangely shy blue dragon. She nested now on the results of those unions. And though she loved her unborn clutch with great passion, her love for Max was undiminished.

"Oink, oink, quack, quack, moo, moo, all

fall down!" sang Max in a high sweet voice as he nestled between her great forelegs. Tecla did not quite understand his words, but she sighed with contentment and watched him through half-closed eyes.

Suddenly the dragon felt a shaft of pain rip through her belly and she quivered with the shock. As the tremor passed, Max stopped singing and gazed into her eyes.

"What's the matter, don't you like my song?" he asked. The pain did not return and after a moment the dragon urged him to continue with a soft flick of her tongue.

"I know Father thinks the black egg is going to be biggest and strongest," said Max, "but I like the blue egg best. It's special and I think it needs me more. I bet it'll be just as good as the black egg when it hatches. I wonder what it'll look like. I can hardly wait for them to hatch. I hope it happens soon.

"Oh, I forgot! I saved you some honey bread," said Max. He held up a gray clay bowl whose interior was glazed a bright sky blue. Seated on the broad gray rim was a fat brown clay bear who wore a permanent smile.

"Father said we could bring one special thing and I brought my bowl. Lydia said I was a baby, but I don't care. Here, eat this before it gets the nest sticky."

But the dragon turned from the treat and lay her head on the edge of the nest.

"What's the matter?" asked Max. "You love honey bread."

Just then another spasm tore through the dragon. This time she grunted with the pain.

"What's wrong?" Max asked in alarm. "Something's wrong! I'm going to get help!" And clambering out of the nest, he hurried toward the alcove.

"Lydia, come quick!" cried Max. "Something's wrong with Tecla!"

"Oh, Max, what could be wrong with a dragon?"

"Lydia, I mean it! Something's wrong with Tecla. She's hurting!" cried Max as he tugged at his sister's arm.

The urgency in Max's tone caused her to look at him and the fear in his eyes showed that he was serious. She jumped to her feet and quickly followed him to the nest. One glance at Tecla convinced her that something *was* wrong with the beast.

"Do dragons get stomach aches?" she asked nervously.

"No," said Max. He wriggled under the enormous head so he could cradle it in his lap. "Father says dragons have stomachs like iron, that's why they can eat almost anything. It's something else. Look, her eyes are closed and she's hardly even trying to hold her head up. Lydia, I'm scared. She's not going to . . . to die, is she?"

"Don't be silly," said Lydia, brushing a long strand of hair from her face. But in truth she was worried. The dragon's head lolled at an awkward angle and harsh breaths rasped from her throat.

"Max, go down to the edge of the pass and see if Father and Daniel are in sight," said Lydia.

Sliding out from under the heavy head, Max crawled down from the nest and raced for the entrance to the cave. As soon as he stepped out onto the high ledge, the wind caught him. It plucked at him hungrily, pulling him toward the abyss.

Max fought the surging winds and inched himself forward to the safety of the pass. The wind wailed around him in eerie, high-pitched tones, singing of fear and death.

Max trembled, but his love for the dragon was greater than his fright and he closed his ears to the singing winds.

Even though he went as far as the pasture, there was no sign of his father. Holding a clump of grass before him, he lured his pony toward a small boulder where he mounted with difficulty.

More than an hour had passed before he

halted the pony. "Oh, pony, what should I do?" he whispered. "They could be any-where. There's lots of little side valleys with tall grass. Maybe they didn't go all the way to the bottom. Maybe I passed them. They could be back at the cave by now. Maybe I should go back.

"They're not here," he whispered in despair when the pasture was once more be-fore him. "But maybe Tecla's better! Maybe everything's all right!" and he slid off the pony's back.

The wind still crooned its deadly song and tried its best to nudge Max off the ledge, but his mind was fixed on the dragon and he barely heard its cries.

The silence of the cave was startling after the shrill keening of the wind. Max hurried forward and climbed into the nest with Lydia and the dragon.

"I couldn't find them," he said. "Is Tecla any better?" But even as he spoke, he could see that she was not.

Lydia was stroking the great beast. "I think she's sleeping now. She doesn't move when I call."

"Sleeping?" asked Max. "She doesn't look like this when she sleeps. Look how her head's dangling! Lydia, we've got to do something!"

"What?" Lydia asked helplessly. "I've said a prayer to Hespus. I don't know what else to do."

"Sing," said Max. "Maybe she can hear us. We'll just have to keep singing and talking to her until Father gets back; he'll know what to do."

8

Attack

But Godwin and Daniel were far away and it was many hours before they returned. Entering the cave, they were struck by the rank odor of sickness even before Lydia hurried over to them.

"I'm so glad you're back," she whispered. "Something's wrong with Tecla. She's sick."

Godwin flung down his armload of hay and rushed to the nest. The dragon lay slumped across her eggs, her great head sprawled on Max's lap. Godwin climbed into the nest and gently drew back a scaled eyelid. The dragon's eye stared without recognition and her body was cool to the touch.

"How long has she been like this?" Godwin asked as he watched another spasm twist her belly.

"Since right after you left," said Max in a voice choked with tears. "I tried to find you but I couldn't. Will she be all right, Father?"

"I'll save her if it's the last thing I do," said Godwin, leaping down from the nest.

"What's the matter with her, Father?" Daniel asked quietly. "Has she ever been sick before?"

"No," said Godwin through tight lips. "But maybe it's more than that. Maybe she's been poisoned. I didn't think Iestyn would carry his hatred so far. Perhaps I was wrong.

"Lydia," he yelled, "fill the large kettle with water and get a sack of valerian and two sacks of golden seal. Daniel, start a large fire and help your sister with the kettle."

"What should I do?" cried Max. "I want to help!"

"You're doing the best thing right where you are," said Godwin. "Keep talking to her. Let her know you're there."

They worked feverishly, building up the fire till it roared. When the kettle was boiling, they pulled it off the fire and put the dried herbs in to steep. Then they strained the fragrant brew through a clean white cloth and did their best to pour it down the dragon's throat.

At first it seemed as though the potion might work, for the dragon roused and roared with pain, but then she fell back weakly and did not respond to their cries.

"We've done all we can," Godwin said as midnight neared. He wiped his brow with an arm that shook with fatigue. "It's in the hands of the Gods now. If she lasts the night, perhaps she'll survive. Go to bed. I'll keep watch."

Daniel and Lydia collapsed on their sleeping mats still fully clothed, barely managing a prayer for the dragon before they fell into an exhausted sleep. Max remained where he was at the dragon's head.

"You too, Max," said Godwin. "There's nothing you can do for her now. I don't even think she knows you're there."

"No," said Max in a quiet but determined voice. "I'll stay here. If she wakes up, she'll know that I'm with her. It will make her feel better."

"Who am I to argue?" said Godwin. "You may well be right. Stay there then, and let me know if there's any change."

He crossed to the firepit and stoked it high with the few logs that remained. Then he tucked his sword close to his side and settled down with his back against the nest.

Almost against his will, his eyes closed. He shook his head and rubbed his heavy lids, but the day had exhausted him. Soon his breath grew deep and his chin rested on his chest as he slept.

Throughout the long night Max sat at the dragon's head and listened as her breath grew shallow and weak.

"Do not leave me," he pleaded in the silent secret passage of thoughts that he and the dragon had shared since earliest days. But the dragon was far from his reach and he could not touch her mind. Grieving, he hugged the great head to his heart. "I will not let you go," he whispered fiercely. "You cannot leave me." And his heart leaped as a tiny whisper brushed his mind.

"Try! Try!" Max whispered jubilantly. "I am here! I won't leave you!" And the thin thread of willpower that had kept the dragon from death began to draw her back toward life.

It was Max who heard them first, in the empty gray-black space before dawn. Perhaps it was the small, soft creak of a wagon wheel or the rattle of a stone that alerted him. Even as a cry of alarm formed in his throat, the invaders were inside the cavern. There were eight of them, just visible in the light of the dying fire.

Seven of them were strangers but the last was well known to Max. Iestyn!

"Father!" called Max. Instantly Godwin

was on his feet, turning an anxious face toward the nest.

"No, Father, the entrance!" cried Max. At the sound of his voice, the men, who seemed almost as surprised as Max, flung themselves forward.

Godwin turned, uttered a cry to Hespus and all the Gods. Then he ripped his sword from its scabbard as the first men lunged at him with blades drawn.

Max screamed and the dragon stirred weakly. At the sound of their brother's voice, Daniel and Lydia sat up and stared with astonishment at the men who were running toward them.

"Run, Daniel!" yelled Godwin, sidestepping a thrust.

But Daniel stood stunned while Iestyn and his men filled the cavern, waving their swords and yelling cries of victory.

An evil leer creased Malac's bearded face as he reached for Lydia. Breaking free of the numbing shock that held her, Lydia grabbed a jug of oil that stood next to the firepit and threw it at Malac's face. It bounced off his chest and fell to the ground and broke. He was roaring with laughter when the oil splashed onto his clothes and spilled into the fire. But his laughter turned to shrieks of terror when the fire exploded outward and covered his body in flames. Screaming hor-

ribly, he fell to the floor and rolled about, trying frantically to extinguish the blaze.

Daniel snapped out of his daze. With a quick prayer to Hespus, he seized his father's short sword, which lay next to his sleeping mat, and he ran to the nest, ready to battle at Godwin's side.

"Get out of here!" said Godwin as three of the men began to close in. "I'll hold them off as long as possible. Take the black egg and your brother and sister and go!"

"I'm not leaving you," said Daniel as the men edged closer.

"Do as I say!" ordered Godwin. "This is no time for heroics!" Yelling loudly, he flung himself at the attackers with sword held high. Taken by surprise, they fell back and Godwin darted past them.

"Come on, you scum!" he hollered, luring them away from the nest. "Let me teach you what fighting's all about!"

Daniel turned to the nest with fear thick in his throat. "Come down!" he cried to Max over the sounds of clashing steel. "Father says we must go."

"I'm not going," said Max, clinging to the dragon. "Go without me!"

"You're going!" insisted Daniel. Suddenly Lydia appeared at his side. Grabbing her arm, Daniel climbed into the nest and pulled her after him.

"We have to obey Father," gasped Daniel as he struggled to lift the huge black egg. "And he says we're to go!"

"You're not going anywhere," said a harsh voice. And turning, Daniel saw that the fight was over.

There, in front of the nest, wearing a cocky smile, stood Iestyn. Behind him, dangling limply in the grip of two large men, with blood streaming from a cut on his head, was Godwin. A third man was pointing a knife at Godwin's throat.

"Come down from there now," ordered Iestyn, "or your father will die."

Lydia cried out and clutched Daniel's arm. Daniel's eyes blazed. Casting off his sister's hand, he fingered the edge of his blade. Max shivered and huddled closer to the dragon.

"Get down!" thundered Iestyn. "You're not going anywhere and neither are the eggs. They're all mine now!"

9

Fight
and
Flight

Gazing helplessly at their captured father, the frightened children did not budge from the nest. For the moment Iestyn ignored them.

"Let's get those eggs out," he said as his men gathered round him.

"Hold on," said Olwen. "What about the dragon? And the Dragonlord? You said he wouldn't be here and there was never no mention of children."

"Forget the dragon; she's just dead meat," said Iestyn. "As for our friends here, a slight miscalculation, but no real problem. We'll just take them with us when we leave and sell them to the Sea Folk. I hear they always need new rowers, since the old ones die so fast."

"Aye, that would work," Weylin said with a smirk. He held his knife even closer to Godwin's throat, as if daring the Dragonlord to move. "Sell them to the Sea Folk, a proper comedown for the high and mighty."

"Kray, bring in the wagon," ordered Iestyn, and the man hurried to obey. Soon the wagon, unhitched from the horses and piled high with lowland hay, sat inside the mouth of the cave.

"Ulpha! Olwen! Get up in the nest and get those eggs!" barked Iestyn.

"Me?" asked Ulpha, looking at the dragon with apprehension. "What if she's not dead?"

"She's dead," snarled Iestyn. He drew his sword and moved toward his henchman. "I made sure of that. You're not afraid, are you?"

"No, I guess not," Ulpha said slowly, eyeing the keen-edged blade. "She looks dead enough." Reluctantly, he climbed into the nest. Another wave of the sword and he was joined by Olwen.

Daniel and Lydia backed away from the advancing men. But Max remained at the side of the dragon, hugging her tightly and staring in wide-eyed terror.

"Hand down those eggs," instructed Iestyn. "And be sure you don't miss any."

"How are we supposed to get at them?" asked Olwen. "She's lying on some of them."

"I don't care how you do it," said Iestyn. "Tip her out of the nest if you have to. Just get those eggs!"

"Touch that dragon and you're all dead men!" said a weak voice. Turning, Iestyn saw that Godwin had pulled himself erect between his captors.

"You forget that you're not giving the orders around here anymore," snarled Iestyn. "I am."

Godwin struggled weakly, but Iestyn just laughed and nodded to the little man with the knife. "Watch him, Weylin, he's all yours now. Wulf, you and Quinby can load the wagon."

Turning his attention back to the nest, Iestyn said, "Ulpha! Olwen! Start with that big black one. Kray! Get up in the wagon and pad it well!"

Ignoring the children, Ulpha and Olwen began to hand the eggs down, rummaging under the dragon's body for the last of them, until all but the blue egg nestled in the wagon.

"You don't want this little funny-looking one, do you?" asked Ulpha as he prodded the blue egg with his foot.

"No, leave it," said Iestyn. "It won't hatch and we have enough. Now tie up the brats and toss them down too."

Olwen reached back and grabbed Lydia by the shoulder. "I'll take care of this one," he said with a grim smile. "To pay for poor Malac."

But almost before he had finished speaking, Lydia spat full in his face and bit the hand that clutched her shoulder. As Olwen shrieked in pain, Lydia kicked him in the shins, leaped over the edge of the nest and ran.

Daniel was quick to follow his sister's lead and rammed his fists into Ulpha's soft stomach. Ulpha gave a startled grunt and doubled over, gasping for breath. Scooping up his short sword from where it had fallen, Daniel hesitated for only a second before plunging it into the heart of his would-be captor. Then, ripping the sword free, he too leaped from the nest.

Iestyn screamed with rage and waved his sword.

"Grab those children!" he cried as Daniel and Lydia rushed in opposite directions.

Several men started to obey, but they were too slow. The children had already slipped off into the shadows deep in the cave.

"I've got this one!" cried Olwen as he

reached for Max, who still huddled at the dragon's side.

"Give him to me," said Iestyn. "A little of his blood should end this nonsense."

But Max clung fiercely to the dragon and was removed only by force. Kicking and crying, he was handed to Iestyn, who held him at arm's length for all to see.

"Come back here now," he called loudly to Lydia and Daniel. "Or I'll kill him."

Then, before anyone could move, the dragon stirred.

"She lives! The dragon is alive!" screamed Kray as he jumped off the wagon.

"Kill her, Olwen!" screamed Iestyn.

"*No!*" yelled Max, struggling wildly.

And then it happened. As Olwen raised his sword for the killing blow, Tecla lifted her head and loosed a blast of flame.

Quinby, Wulf and Kray were engulfed by the fire, which then reached out for Iestyn. As the blaze wrapped around the left side of his body, he fell to the ground, dropping Max. Max ran back to the nest and leaped at Olwen just as his sword struck the dragon.

The screams mingled, those of Iestyn and the dragon and the unfortunate Olwen, who was crushed when the dragon rolled upon him in her death throes.

"No! *No!*" cried Max, hurling himself on

the dragon, trying to stop the flow of blood. But it was too late. Feeling her life seeping from her, the dragon gazed at the small child. Her tongue flicked his face one last time and then was still.

A great numbness filled Max as he lay pressed against the dragon. Dimly he heard Godwin yell. The Dragonlord had broken free and found his sword; one slash drove Weylin back and then Godwin advanced on Iestyn.

Iestyn staggered to his feet, horribly burned over the left side of his body. He gripped his sword with shaking hands and circled, seeking an enemy he could barely see.

"Where are you!" he screamed, straining to see with puffy, flame-seared eyes. "Come here!" he shrieked wildly. "You'll not escape me!"

"Here I am," Godwin said hoarsely, stepping in front of Iestyn. "Prepare to die!"

"You'll not stop me!" raged Iestyn. "Not this time!" and he slashed out with his sword, narrowly missing Godwin.

"To the death!" cried Godwin, and the battle began.

Back and forth they fought. First one pressed the advantage, then the other, with Weylin hovering nearby. Godwin should have been an easy winner, for other than the blow that had stunned him, he was unhurt, and he had the longer reach. But Iestyn's hatred gave the injured man a strength and fury that evened the odds.

"Weylin!" cried Iestyn, and the man with the knife slipped up behind Godwin. But the children also responded to his call.

Running out from behind the nest, Daniel blocked Weylin's attack with the short sword and defended his father's back.

Lydia dashed to the top of a gold mound and threw coins, hard as hail, at Godwin's assailants.

Safe in the nest, Max watched the battle through grief-filled eyes.

Weapons clashing, the combatants crashed into the wagon. Curses flew and muscles strained as each man attempted to throw the other off balance and drive home the killing blow. Godwin and Iestyn surged back and forth, bumping against the side of the egg-filled wagon. It was almost impossible to tell one from the other, so tightly were they locked in each other's grip. And always Weylin danced around them, easily avoiding Daniel's blows and Lydia's missiles as he waited for the chance to strike.

Once and then twice the two foes shoved against the wagon, and then someone uttered a terrible cry as it rocked on its wheels. Slowly, slowly it tilted. And then, even as hands reached to hold it, the wagon fell with a crash, spewing the eggs out onto the hard rock floor.

Weylin gave a cry of despair and rushed around the overturned wagon. "They're all broken!" he shrieked. "Every last one of them! All is for nothing!"

Whirling with the speed of desperation, Weylin flung his knife at Godwin, who stood free of Iestyn, staring in horror at the terrible sight. Daniel yelled a warning. But it was too late. The knife thudded home, burying itself deep in Godwin's chest.

"Father!" cried Daniel, catching Godwin's body as it crumpled to the ground.

"Father?" said Daniel. Lydia suddenly appeared and flung herself at Weylin, clawing at his eyes and pulling his hair. Iestyn stood staring at the blood that welled from Godwin's chest, dazed and disbelieving. Max buried his head in his arms and wept.

Godwin opened his eyes and tried to smile at Daniel. "Take the blue egg and go," he gasped. "Find the tunnel. Protect your brother and sister. You are the Dragonlord. Go. I love you."

As Daniel watched, a stillness settled on Godwin. An awful, flat gaze stole over his clear gray eyes, and Daniel knew that his father was dead.

It seemed to Daniel that the world stopped

in that moment. Somewhere outside himself, he knew that Iestyn now knelt beside him, and that Lydia still fought with Weylin, but it didn't matter. For a time he could draw no air and the lump in his throat was like a stone. Then he took a ragged breath, and the world began again.

"He's dead!" Iestyn said in wonder. "He's really dead! But—but I never really meant for him to die. I just wanted to win, and to make him suffer."

Leaving the stunned Iestyn beside his father's body, Daniel climbed to his feet and went to aid his sister. Weylin had her by the hair and was fumbling in his belt for a second knife. Daniel smashed his short sword down on Weylin's head and the man fell, blood streaming from a gash on his skull.

Daniel seized his sister's wrist and the two of them ran back to the nest, skirting the bodies of the burned men. Clambering over the dead dragon, Daniel grabbed Max and shook him hard. "Come," he said. "We must take the blue egg and go. Father said so."

"Father?" asked Max, raising a tear-stained face.

"He's dead," Lydia said stiffly. "We're alone now."

"Dead," Max said numbly. "They're both dead."

"And we will be too if we don't leave now," Lydia said savagely.

"Quick!" said Daniel. "The egg!" He grabbed a large wad of the castoff dragonskin and wrapped it around the lumpy blue egg.

"Out, Max!" ordered Lydia. Shoving the stunned child before her, she hastily pushed him over the rear edge of the nest and jumped out after him. Daniel took one last look at his father's body, then scrambled out of the nest carrying the precious egg.

Dragging Max between them, Lydia and Daniel started for the back of the cavern.

"We need food," said Lydia. "Keep going, I'll catch up." And before Daniel could disagree, she darted toward the alcove.

Carefully avoiding the corpse of Malac, she grabbed a sack and began stuffing it with food. Weylin begin to stir as she worked.

"Iestyn, where are the children?" he cried. He staggered up and stumbled around the wagon, his voice filled with panic. "You didn't let them get away, did you? We've got to find them or we're dead men!"

Grabbing some cheese and a sharp knife, Lydia slipped into the shadows and raced after her brothers.

"There they go!" cried Weylin, and he pulled Iestyn to his feet. Ignoring their injuries, the frightened men set off in pursuit.

It seemed to Max that the children were

caught in some great nightmare as they desperately slipped and slithered over the huge mounds of gold. Precious gems rolled beneath their feet, threatening to topple them back down the hills and into the hands of their pursuers. And it was dark. Only the faint light of early dawn lit their way, and they continued more by feel than by sight.

"How much farther?" gasped Lydia.

"I don't know," said Daniel as he stumbled along, holding the bundled egg to his chest. "It seems like the roof's getting lower but it's so dark, I can't tell."

As he reached the top of the last mound, the footing suddenly gave way beneath him. Horrified, Lydia watched him roll to the bottom, dragging Max and the egg with him.

Behind her Lydia could hear the rasping breathing of Iestyn and Weylin. Glancing back, she saw them clawing their way toward her.

"Hurry!" she cried as she ran down the mound and pulled her brothers to their feet. "They're catching up!"

"The egg seems all right," gasped Daniel as he gingerly felt around it. "I don't think it's broken."

"Where's the door?" demanded Lydia. "There's nothing here but solid rock."

"I don't know!" answered Daniel. "I don't know any more than you do."

"It's there on the left," said Max in a heavy voice. Slowly his arm lifted and pointed the way.

"Where? Here? *Yes!* I see it!" exclaimed Daniel, finding a crack in the rock face. "How did you—"

"Never mind that now! Open it, quick!" cried Lydia as Iestyn and Weylin began to slide down the hill of gold.

"It—it won't open!" said Daniel. Frantically he pulled and pried at the rock.

"I must live," said Max in a monotone. Pushing Daniel's hand aside, he touched the rock wall with his fingertips. A stone panel swung aside, revealing total darkness.

"Hurry! Into the tunnel!" cried Lydia, and she shoved her brothers into the pitch-black hole.

"They're getting away!" screamed Weylin.

"Stop them!" shrieked Iestyn, throwing himself forward. "Don't let them escape!"

As Iestyn hurtled down the mound, waving his sword above his head, Max touched the rock panel a second time. It swung shut with a solid thud, sealing Iestyn out, just as surely as it sealed the children in.

10

The Dark Tunnel

The children collapsed in a heap as the heavy rock wall closed behind them. The sounds of hammering and cursing could be heard, though muffled and distant, from the other side.

"Can they get in?" Lydia asked nervously.

"I don't think so," replied Daniel. "But maybe we should leave before they find some way to break the door down. If they really mean to get us, they'll find something in the cave to help them."

"Leave here? Leave Father?" cried Lydia, her self-assurance deserting her.

"Lydia, we can't stay here," said Daniel. "We can't help Father or Tecla. They're dead. Murdered. And we saw it happen.

Iestyn knows he has to catch us. If we escape and tell on him, he'll be hanged."

"But how are we going to get out of here?" Lydia wailed. "It's pitch black. Where will we go? What if we fall in a hole?"

"I know it won't be easy," said Daniel, "but we have to go on. Father told me to take care of you and Max and the egg and with the Gods' help that's what I'm going to do."

"Oh, the egg. I almost forgot!" and she reached out and felt for it. Her questing hand touched a small leg. "Max?" she said hesitantly. But there was only a hiccuping sob.

"Oh, Max," said Lydia as she traced her brother's body. "Are you all right?" And gathering the small child to her, she cradled his head against her chest and rocked him back and forth.

"Don't cry," she said, wiping the tears from his face. "Father wouldn't want us to cry. We must be brave. After all, we're the children of the Dragonlord."

"I'm the Dragonlord," said Daniel.

"Be quiet, Daniel," snapped Lydia. Then, in a softer voice, "Now, Maxie, dry those tears. We've got a job to do and you must help us. We have to find our way out of here and keep the egg alive. You'd like to help with the egg, wouldn't you?"

"Yes," said Max, choking back his tears.

"Good," said Lydia. "Then it will be your job to keep the egg covered at all times. I don't know too much about hatching eggs but I'm sure it needs to stay warm. Can you do that?"

"Yes, I will," said Max. "I promised Tecla."

"What did you promise her?" asked Daniel, but before Max could reply there was renewed battering on the rock wall and the barrier trembled.

"They're still trying to break it down," said Daniel. "We'd better leave. I'll go first and feel the way. If we stay next to the wall, maybe we'll be all right. Lydia, you carry the egg, and Max, you carry the food."

"I'll carry the egg," said Max.

"You can't carry it, Max. It must weigh ten pounds!" said Daniel. "What if you dropped it?"

"I won't drop it," Max said stubbornly. "I have to take care of it, I promised."

"Let him carry it, Daniel," said Lydia. "If it's that important to him, he'll be careful."

"All right," said Daniel, fumbling in the dark for the dragonskin bundle. "But you better not drop it."

Then, with the blows on the door sounding behind them, the children moved forward into the darkness.

It was *totally* dark, without the tiniest

glimmer of light to show the way. Slowly, hesitantly, fearfully, the children felt their way along, one hand to the side touching the wall, feet sliding along the floor, probing for holes. Daniel, in the lead, held his sword before him to prevent walking into a barrier or a suddenly lowered ceiling.

The air, though musty and damp, was breathable. But there were no air currents to indicate access to the outside. Nor were there any noises, other than those made by Iestyn and Weylin, which faded away as the children progressed.

The floor was rough and littered with rock debris, and the walls were equally crude. The ceiling rose and fell irregularly. The tunnel was clearly a natural formation and had not been made by man.

The children traveled slowly, shuffling and stumbling in the dark, each wrapped in private thoughts. Occasionally a sob would echo through the dark tunnel, and they would stop and cling to one another, touching and comforting, lending the strength to continue.

At last they could go no farther. Giving in to grief and exhaustion, the children sank to the rough ground. Shuddering with fear of the dark and the memory of death, Max curled around the egg and quietly sobbed himself to sleep.

"Where do you think this tunnel goes?" Lydia asked, holding back her own tears.

"I don't know," Daniel answered wearily. "It seems to be going down. Maybe it really does come out on the other side of the mountain."

"But that's Bilbergia!" Lydia said in alarm. "They're Gallardia's worst enemy!"

"Well, what choice do we have?" asked Daniel. "Iestyn behind us and Bilbergia in front. Even if we went back and waited till Iestyn left, what then? You know he's going to be waiting for us somewhere. We'd never make it back to town alive."

"How's he going to explain what happened to Father and Tecla and the eggs and us?"

"Lydia, don't you understand? Iestyn doesn't have to explain anything!" Daniel said angrily. "Everyone was killed except him and Weylin. All he has to do is go back to town and wait for someone else to discover the bodies. Then he'll pretend to be as surprised as everyone else. No one will ever know he had anything to do with it!"

"Granny Roone will know! We know!" said Lydia.

"But Lydia, no one will believe Granny Roone! She's old and everyone knows she doesn't like Iestyn. And we can't tell anyone 'cause we're here."

"You mean he's going to get away with it!" cried Lydia, her voice tight with rage.

"Yes," said Daniel. "Unless you can think of something that I've missed."

"He won't get away with murdering Father," said Lydia. "I won't let him!"

"Lydia, I'm as upset as you are," Daniel said grimly. "But we've got to get out of here before we can do anything about Iestyn. When we do, I promise you we'll have our revenge."

"How can you be so calm!" screamed Lydia. "Our father's lying back there, dead! Murdered! And you tell me to forget it! You're scared of Iestyn. You're scared to do anything. You may be a boy, but you don't deserve to be Dragonlord. And if we get out of here, I'm going to do something about it!"

The harsh words echoed in the darkness and then there was silence, broken only by the sound of Max's muffled sobs.

"You don't mean it, Lydia. You're just upset," Daniel said quietly. "And you've wakened Max. Come on, Maxie, settle down. She didn't mean it."

"Yes, I did, Daniel," Lydia said. "I meant every word. And when that egg hatches, I'm going to be the one it bonds with."

"Father told me to be there and that's what I'm going to do," Daniel said in a quiet but firm voice. "I'm Dragonlord and I'm the one it will bond with."

"We'll see," said Lydia. "Get up! We won't get anywhere lying around like this!" Shoving past her brothers, she took the lead.

11

The Glowing Cavern

Wrapped in angry silence and private grief, the children followed the tunnel for a long time. Suddenly Lydia cried out, "Look! Up ahead! Isn't that light?" and they rushed forward, anxious to be free of the terrible clinging darkness.

"Be careful! It might be a trap!" cried Daniel, but Lydia ignored him and plunged ahead to the end of the long tunnel and out into the light.

"Why, it's another cave!" she cried. "A big, wonderful, beautiful, safe cave!"

It was, as she said, a large cave. Its walls rose smooth and sheer to the roof, which shone with a warm, pale light.

"We don't know that it's safe," said Daniel

as he stood blinking in the unexpected brightness.

"Look, Daniel," said Max as he gently lowered the bundled egg to the ground. "The ceiling's glowing."

"It's moving, too!" said Daniel. He peered up at the roof, which seemed to swarm with tiny movement. "And listen to that humming noise. Why, I think it's some kind of lightbug."

"I wouldn't care if they were spiders!" said Lydia. "They make light and that's all that matters."

Then she gazed in wonder at the rest of the cavern. Smooth white sand crunched underfoot and sparkled in the pale light. To her great relief, the sand held no sign of footprints, either animal or human. Far in the distance on the opposite wall, she saw the dark mouths of other caves or tunnels.

Sitting down on the smooth sand, Lydia opened the food bag and began to take things out. "I'm starving!" she said. "Let's eat. We've got cheese and bread and the last of that roast goat and some sugar."

"Lydia, we can't eat now," said Daniel. "Iestyn could be right behind us. And we need to investigate this place; something dangerous might live here."

"I suppose you're right," Lydia said with a sigh. "What should we do—keep going?"

"No, then we'd always be worrying that Iestyn was somewhere behind us. I think we should close off the tunnel. Then we'd know we were safe—at least from Iestyn."

"How are we going to do that?" asked Lydia as she studied the boulders that surrounded the mouth of the tunnel. "These rocks are too heavy to move and we don't have any tools."

"I don't think we're going to need any," said Daniel. He climbed cautiously onto the boulders. "See this?" he asked, pointing to a long, thin stone that protruded from the rock face. "There's a symbol carved on it. I bet it means something like 'pull this stone.' See how all those big stones are resting on it? It's the key balance point. If we pulled it out, all these rocks would come crashing down and bury the tunnel. Iestyn would never get through."

"And we'd never be able to go back," Lydia said somberly.

"I won't do it unless you agree," said Daniel, "but I think it's dangerous to leave the tunnel open."

"You're right," Lydia said at last. "But I sure hope there's another way out of here. All right. Do it. Pull the stone."

"Not yet," said Daniel. "I'd get squashed if I pulled it with my hand. Give me the laces from your bodice; Max, give me your belt."

"Don't look," said Lydia primly, and turning her back, she unlaced her bodice and handed the long red ribbon to Max. Max added his own blue belt and tossed the two to Daniel, who tied them into one long length. Then he attached it to the end of the stone and scrambled down to the ground. "Back up," he said. "I don't know how far the rocks will fall." Drawing the ribbon taut, he yanked it sharply. The balance stone came free and landed in the sand at his feet.

At first nothing happened. Then there was a low growling noise, as though the earth itself were moaning. Then came a wrenching shriek that filled the cavern, causing the glowing bugs to shift and flutter. And then the rocks came down.

"Get back!" screamed Daniel. "The whole thing's going!"

When the cloud of dust cleared at last, the children saw that the tunnel entrance was buried beneath a tremendous pile of broken rock.

"We'll never get through there now," Lydia said tremulously, as she took back her ribbon.

"No," agreed Daniel, "but neither will Iestyn. Now why don't you two make a camp while I look around and make sure we're not in any danger."

"Go ahead," said Lydia. "I'll feed Max."

The murmur of running water caught Daniel's ear as he left his brother and sister. Drawing the short sword, he approached a pile of boulders that lay far along the wall to the right of the blocked tunnel. When he rounded the pile, he saw rivulets of water trickling down the rock face and splashing over fallen rocks into a small round pool set in the sand.

The cool wet sounds drew the boy to the edge of the pool. As he peered into the water he saw small glowing fish swimming in its crystal depths. Between the pool and the wall, pale fleshy ferns had rooted in the damp sand and were growing in great profusion. Tiny white salamanders with jewellike red eyes watched without fear beneath the spray-drenched fronds.

Dipping his hand into the pool, Daniel sniffed the water and tasted a drop carefully before drinking his fill.

"I found water," he said as he rejoined his brother and sister.

"Good," said Lydia. "We'll need some when we wake up."

"Maxie, something's been bothering me," Daniel said as he sat down next to his brother.

"What?" Max asked sleepily.

"How did you know where that secret door was? I certainly couldn't see it."

"I wondered about that too," said Lydia.

"Oh," Max said between yawns, "the egg told me."

"Max, I'll pinch your head if you fib," snapped Lydia.

"I'm not lying. The egg told me," said Max, and almost before he had finished speaking, his eyes closed.

"Is that possible?" asked Daniel.

"How do I know?" said Lydia. "You're the big dragon expert around here. You tell me."

"I'm no expert, Lydia. I never said I knew everything."

"Well, at least we agree on something," said Lydia. She lay down on the soft sand and hugged her arms against her chest to ward off the chill of the cave. "I'm going to sleep," she said. "I'm tired. But since you're the Dragonlord now, you can stay awake and protect us."

"Certainly," said Daniel with a small bow, "although I suspect whatever might roam these tunnels is in more danger from you."

Flipping her long hair over her shoulder, Lydia glared furiously at her brother, then turned her back and hunched into an angry ball.

After Lydia's breathing had relaxed in deep sleep, Max opened his eyes. "Why is she being so mean?" he whispered to Daniel.

"I don't know," said his brother, sighing. "I guess she's angry at me for being in charge. And I'm sure she's upset about Father. You know she hates to cry; she'd rather get mad. Never mind, Maxie. Tell me, how's the egg?"

"I don't know," said Max. He pulled aside a flap of the dragonskin. "Eggs are supposed to stay warm. Do you think it's warm enough?"

Daniel hooked his thumbs through his belt and studied the egg with a critical eye. It sat on the folds of skin like a large lumpy blue pumpkin and was neither warm nor cool to the touch.

"Why don't we move it next to Lydia? Then all three of us can sleep next to it. If we pull the dragonskin over us, we'll all stay warm," said Daniel.

"Will it be all right then?" Max asked anxiously.

Daniel wrapped his arms around Max's thin shoulders and looked with concern at the dark smudges of fatigue that lay under the little boy's eyes.

"Yes," he said, trying to keep the worry from his voice. "I'm sure everything will be fine."

"Are Father and Tecla really dead, Daniel?" asked Max, his face pinched and white. "Maybe they were only hurt. Maybe they're still alive."

"No, Max, they're dead," Daniel said gently. "I wouldn't have left them if they'd been alive. Try not to think about it." He smoothed the silky brown hair back from the little face. And as tears filled his own eyes, he hugged his brother tightly and said in a husky voice, "Everything will be better tomorrow."

12

An Amazing Discovery

Pain and rage tore at Iestyn as he pounded on the rock.

"We've got to get it open!" he screamed at the little man who stood beside him. "We can't let those children escape!" Iestyn drew his sword and smashed it against the wall repeatedly, but the rock did not give. Then he jabbed the wall with the sword point. It lodged in a crack and the man grunted with satisfaction, realizing he'd found the secret door. But when he tried to lever it open, the blade snapped. Iestyn bellowed with frustration and beat on the wall with the hilt.

"Back to the wagon!" said Weylin. "Maybe we can find a tool, a length of metal to help us pry it open."

"I don't know if I can make it," groaned

Iestyn, leaning against the rock wall. "My skin feels as though it's still on fire and I can hardly see."

"Stuff your whining," said Weylin. "I have no pity for you. It's your fault we're in this mess. You said the Dragonlord and his brats were away. You said we'd never see them. You said the dragon would be dead. Well, look at us now, blacksmith. Wulf's dead and Ulpha and all the others too. And for what? The eggs are all broken, save the one the children took, and the Dragonlord and the dragon are dead. And once it's known what we've done, we're dead men. This is a hanging offense in Gallardia."

"But who's to tell?" argued Iestyn as Weylin fingered his knife. "You and I are the only ones left and we won't talk. And there's the gold. There's enough wealth here for us to live like kings wherever we choose."

"Don't be a fool," snapped Weylin as he began climbing the mound of gold, heading back to the entrance. "We could load the wagon with gold and jewels. We might even make it over the mountains and into Bilbergia. But what then? The Bilbergian army patrols constantly and they don't like strangers."

"We'll bribe them!" cried Iestyn, trying desperately to keep up.

"Why should they take a bribe when they

could have everything?" said Weylin. "It was different when there were eight of us, but now there's only two. They'll just kill us and take the wagon. And even if we do escape them somehow, we'll still be marked men. Sooner or later this mess will be discovered. Then someone will miss us and everyone will know we did it. No, we have only one chance of getting out of this alive."

"What?" asked Iestyn as he scrambled alongside.

"Leave everything the way it is and go back to town. Then, when the bodies are discovered, pretend to know nothing."

"I could say I had an accident at the forge," said Iestyn. "I could say that a spark caught my shirt and blazed up before I could put it out."

"Yes," said Weylin as they struggled up the last mound of gold. "But we must be sure of each other. If one of us talks, we will both be dead men. We are linked from this day on as though we were chained."

"Agreed," said Iestyn, and eyeing each other somberly, the two shook hands. Then, ignoring the carnage that surrounded them, they began their search for a tool. As they came to the overturned wagon, the first rays of the rising sun cleared the snowy peaks to the east and flooded the cave with red.

"Over here," said Weylin as he picked his

way through the broken eggs. "Maybe we can undo the wagon shaft and use it as a wedge. Come help me."

Using their knives, they set to work on the long ironclad pole. At last they were rewarded by the groan of ripping wood, and the shaft fell free of the wagon and clattered to the ground.

Iestyn hurried after it as it rolled along the cave floor, and then he stopped abruptly and stared into the deep shadows that bracketed the entrance of the cave. Peering through swollen eyes, he advanced slowly, as though afraid that what he saw would disappear.

"Here! What's the delay?" snapped Weylin. "If we're going to—What! An egg! An unbroken egg!" he whispered in amazement.

"It's mine!" snarled Iestyn as he turned to face Weylin. "Don't even touch it!"

"You're wrong, mate," said Weylin with a smile. "This makes all the difference. So long as there was no other way, I didn't mind if both of us went back empty-handed, but this changes everything. We'll load the wagon with gold and jewels and this egg. If we're stopped and bribes don't work, we'll sell the egg to the Bilbergians. We'll tell them we know how to hatch it. That'll stop them from taking it from us. Then, once they pay us, we slip away. We'll be rich and we'll be safe."

"No," Iestyn whispered hoarsely. "This egg is mine. I knew it as soon as I saw it."

"Oho, so that's how it is, is it?" said Weylin, and his hand tightened on his blade.

"Yes," snarled Iestyn. "That's how it is." With a movement almost too swift to follow, he lashed out with the pole, striking Weylin in the head. The little man staggered off balance, trying to stem the gush of blood that poured from his scalp with one hand and raising his knife with the other. Iestyn sprang forward and, even as Weylin threw his blade, struck the little man with the end of the pole and thrust him out of the cave and off the edge of the mountain.

As Weylin's screams echoed through the pass, Iestyn stumbled back into the cave and sat down with a thump. He stared dumbly at the hilt of the knife that protruded from a point high on his chest where the arm joined the body.

"I shall not die," he whispered. He looked over at the black egg, which glowed faintly in the early morning light. "I cannot die or my whole life has been in vain." Fixing his gaze on the egg, which seemed to pulse with power and promise, he grasped the knife and pulled.

The high, thin cry of an eagle wakened him some time later. "I had to do it. You understand," he whispered to the egg. "I could

not share you or sell you. We will be as one, you and I. I feel it. It was meant to be."

Somehow he pulled himself to his feet and, ignoring his pain, staggered forward. Forcing his burned hand to obey him, he righted the fallen wagon, replaced the shaft and heaped the wagon with hay.

The egg filled his mind and in his delirious state it took on a power of its own that seemed to command him, telling him what to do.

He could never remember lifting the egg into the wagon and dragging the vehicle back through the pass to where he had left the horses. Nor did he remember harnessing the team and hitching them to the wagon. The ride itself was blurred and warped by his fever-ridden mind. He dropped the reins often, allowing the horses to stop while he fainted with pain and drifted in a world of nightmares.

It was late night when he reached the valley and there were no lights to guide him as he entered the sleeping town. With the last traces of strength and sense, he guided the team home.

Lights came on in the windows of his house as he unhitched the team and struggled with the door to his forge. Worried cries rang out behind him.

"Iestyn, where have you been! What has

happened to you!" his wife cried in horror when she saw his wounds. Dimly he heard his son calling his name and felt him pulling gently at his arm. Cursing violently, he threw his son from him and pulled the wagon into the building.

"Leave me alone," he muttered between dry, cracked lips. "Go away!"

"Iestyn!" sobbed his wife. "What's happened?"

"Go away, woman. I don't want you here. Obey me or I will kill you!" and as the madness and pain swirled around him, he closed the door and barred it from within.

13

Footprints in the Sand

"What is this poking into my back?" grumbled Lydia, awakening from a full night's sleep.

"Oh, it's the egg," Daniel answered sleepily. "Max and I put it there so we could keep it warm while we slept."

"No, it's not. Not unless it's grown some horns," said Lydia. She sat up and pushed away the dragonskin that Daniel had draped over her and the egg.

"Why, it's that stupid bear bowl!" cried Lydia. She stared in amazement at the tiny bear perched on top of the bright blue bowl. "And it's full of honey bread. How did it get here?"

"I had it in the nest," said Max, his voice still thick with sleep. "I was trying to get

Tecla to eat some honey bread when she got sick. I guess it fell into the dragonskin."

"It's all sticky. Get rid of it!"

"No, I'll carry it," said Max, and he scrambled to his feet and rescued it from his sister's hands. "You can have some," he said, offering the sticky bowl to his sister and brother.

"Ugh!" Lydia said with a grimace.

"Thanks, but I think I'll eat some cheese," said Daniel.

As they ate, Daniel asked, "Did you notice how warm it was under that dragonskin? I think the skin must have some magical powers. It's so cool in this cave I thought we'd be cold, but the skin kept us all warm, and the egg as well."

"I don't think it's magic," said Lydia. "But dragonskin must be special all on its own. After all, it has to protect the dragon from fire. I wonder if it can do anything besides hold in heat." She picked up the skin and looked at it.

"Why, it's still warm! Feel it, Daniel!"

"You're right," said Daniel as he fingered the filmy gray dragonskin. "I'm going to wrap it around the egg again. Maybe it will keep the egg warm."

"I wish it was magic," said Max. "Then I'd wish that everything was all right and that Father and Tecla were still alive."

"We all would, Max," said Daniel. "And I'd wish that we could find the way out of here. What would you wish for, Lydia?"

"I'd wish to be Dragonlord," Lydia said defiantly. "I'd be a good one."

Daniel and Lydia locked gazes for a long moment, then Daniel broke away and said, "Max, wait here a minute. Lydia and I are going to take a little walk."

Daniel led his sister farther out into the cave, then stopped and turned to her. "We've got to settle this. We can't be fighting all the time. We have to work together or we'll never get out of here. I know you're angry that I'm Dragonlord, but what can I do? Father told me to take care of you and Max and the egg. He told me I was the Dragonlord. I didn't ask for it."

"Well, I *am* asking," said Lydia. "Why don't you let me do it?"

"I can't, Lydia," Daniel said unhappily. "I have to obey Father."

"Why?" asked Lydia, her body taut. "Who would know?"

"I would know," said Daniel. "I'm sorry. Look, I know you're unhappy and that you don't like me, but what can I do about it?"

"It's not that I don't like you," Lydia said in a small voice. "It's just that you act like you know everything. And you never listen to me. I know lots of things too!"

"I'm sorry," said Daniel. "I'll try to be different."

"Oh, stop being so nice!" cried Lydia. "I hate it when you're being nice! All right! I'll do as you say, because I don't want to die down here. But don't think I'll forget about being Dragonlord, 'cause I won't!"

"Fair enough," said Daniel. "We can talk again, once we've found the way out."

After the children had gathered their few possessions, they examined the egg for signs of hatching, but its lumpy blue shell remained unbroken. They wrapped it once more in the dragonskin.

"Well, how do we get out of here?" asked Lydia.

"I think we should follow the water," said Daniel, nodding toward the little pool and the tiny stream that flowed from it. "That stream must go somewhere. Maybe it leads outside."

"What about those?" asked Lydia, pointing to several dark openings that lay on the far side of the cavern. "They might be tunnels."

"They could be," agreed Daniel. "I didn't explore them. I was too tired."

"I think we should explore the entire cave," said Lydia. "We might find something important, like a clue showing which way we should go."

"Like a signpost?" Daniel asked humorously.

"Why not!" Lydia said. "We already found one sign, didn't we? Somebody left that symbol on the balance rock back by the tunnel. Now we know the old stories are really true. This is the secret way through the mountains and other people have been here before us. Maybe they left something else that could help us."

"You could be right," Daniel said.

"You agree with me?" Lydia said in amazement.

"Sure! It's a good idea," said Daniel. "But let's leave the egg by the pool. If we have to stay here again, it will make a better campsite." Daniel led the way to the pool, adding, "I bet we could even catch some of those fish I saw. Come on, I'll show them to you."

"I fish better than you do," said Lydia. "But what are we going to use for—oh!" she gasped. "What's that!"

There in the wet sand at the edge of the pool were tracks. Large tracks with the mark of long thin toes and the prick of claws.

Without speaking, the children drew together and stared in horror. The tracks led to the water and then returned, disappearing in the soft dry sand. Even as they watched, water seeped into the tracks and dissolved them. The creature that had made them had obviously been here only a short time before.

"May the Gods save us," whispered Lydia as she looked around in fear.

14

The Underground River

"What could have made a footprint that big?" whispered Daniel. "I've never seen anything like it before."

"If those are caves over there, it probably lives in them and comes here to drink," said Lydia.

"Do you think it eats people?" asked Max.

"I don't know," Daniel said quietly, "but we'd best be careful. We can't stay here now, it might come back. I think we should go in the opposite direction and follow the stream. What do you think?"

"I think we should go now and stop talking," whispered Lydia. "Maybe it has good hearing."

Moving quietly, the children hurried

along the bank of the tiny stream, fearfully eyeing the distant caves on their left. When Max began to fall behind, Daniel took the heavy egg and slung it over his shoulder. "You can have it back as soon as we get out of here," he said when Max started to protest. "There's nothing wrong with taking turns."

The roof of the cave began to slope downward and the children could plainly see the living mat of insects that covered its surface. They were as big as a man's thumb, with hard, shiny black bodies and stiff, transparent wings. The bottom half of their bodies emitted a pale greenish-white light that flickered on and off. A soft hum rose from the dense mass, which quivered with constant motion.

Ahead of them the roof of the cavern swept down in a majestic curve, joining the soft sand in a jumble of fallen rocks. The stream flowed silently into a dark opening in the wall and disappeared as though it had been swallowed.

Daniel peered into the gloomy opening. "There's some sort of path running along the edge of the water," he said. "I think it's wide enough for us to walk on."

"It's so dark," Max said fearfully. "Do we have to?"

"Max is right," said Lydia. "It's foolish to go in there if we can't see where we're going. I think we should make a torch."

"How? We didn't bring any firestones," replied Daniel.

"Why don't we use the bugs?" said Max. "They make light."

"That's a good idea!" Daniel said. "If we had a stick, maybe they'd attach themselves to it. Then we'd have a torch!"

"What about this?" said Lydia, and she tugged a long, thin stone free of the surrounding rocks.

"Perfect!" said Daniel.

He took the stone and scraped it gently along the curve of the roof. The lights flickered wildly and the insects hummed louder as the stone passed among them, but none clung to its surface.

"Dogsbreath! Give it to me!" Lydia said with exasperation. But she fared no better.

"We could stick them on," she said, staring thoughtfully upward. "If we scraped Max's bear bowl, maybe we could get enough honey to stick them on like glue."

Using the point of Lydia's knife, Daniel scraped the bowl and carefully daubed the stone with dots of honey. Then he reached toward the milling insects.

"Wait!" whispered Lydia. "What if they bite!"

"It's a chance we have to take," said Daniel. His hand darted forward and plucked one of the fat glowing insects free. The small creature buzzed wildly and its small hooked legs flailed the air. But it didn't bite.

"Whew!" Daniel said with a sigh. "Now let's hope it sticks." Carefully placing the insect on the sticky stone, he pressed down on its back, forcing its abdomen against the honey. The insect wriggled once or twice, braced its legs against the stone and flew away with an angry hum.

"Curses!" cried Daniel. "I thought it would work."

"I know how to fix it," said Lydia. "Catch another one!"

While Daniel seized another of the glowing insects, Lydia quickly worked a thread free from the hem of her skirt.

"Turn it over on its back," she commanded, "so it can't use its legs to push off."

And as the insect buzzed in frustration, Daniel held it in place and Lydia wrapped it with thread, tying it securely to the stone.

"Hooray, it works!" cried Max. "And it's glowing even brighter!"

"Probably because it's mad," said Lydia. "Hurry, catch more. I'll get some more thread."

"This is the strangest looking torch I've

ever seen," said Daniel when they finished the task some time later.

"And it didn't do my skirt any good," Lydia said, looking ruefully at the frayed fabric. "But at least we have light."

"Let's go," said Daniel. "I keep worrying that the monster will come back." He handed the bundled-up egg to Max and the food sack to Lydia. Then, holding the strange torch above his head, he entered the cold, dark tunnel with his sister and brother close behind him.

There was little to see at first, only the narrow path of damp, crumbly sand and the tiny stream. The ceiling allowed passage of the torch, but no more. The rough walls pressed close on either side. After a time, the children noticed that water was oozing from the walls and joining with the stream.

"Steady yourselves against the wall," said Daniel, his voice echoing in the damp darkness. "Hold on so you don't slip."

Max and Lydia needed no urging and they clung to the wall on their left as the footing grew worse. The children took turns carrying the dragonskin bundle.

More and more water trickled from the rocks as they continued hour after dark hour. Moisture filled the air, beading their hair and dampening their clothes. The stream swelled

to a fair-sized river that sped along at a great pace. The ceiling began to climb and the walls drew farther apart, forcing the children to leave the bank.

"Keep next to the wall," Daniel said over the noise of the rippling water. "It's safer. We might fall in if we try to stay by the river."

Then, after a while, the wall turned left quite suddenly, and as far as the children could see, there was nothing but dark emptiness.

"What do we do now?" whispered Max, standing as close to Daniel as he could get.

"Head back to the river," said Daniel after a moment's pause. "We'll just have to be careful. Max, you stay behind me and hold on to my jerkin. Lydia, you follow Max."

They began to slog toward the river, which lay some thirty yards distant. At last it appeared before them, grown to a torrent that roared and snarled as though alive.

"I'm scared," wailed Max as the torch shone on the froth-crested water. "I want to go home!"

"Hush, Maxie, it'll be all right," said Lydia, hugging her brother. But her words were whipped away by the noise of the river, and as she stared at the vicious current she felt her confidence drain away.

"This is close enough!" shouted Daniel. "Any closer and we might slip and fall in. But let's try to go faster."

Holding tightly to each other, they moved along the riverbank at a brisk pace, growing more frightened at every step.

Suddenly Daniel stopped short, causing Max and Lydia to bump into him.

"What now?" Lydia cried peevishly.

"Look!" said Daniel, holding the torch close to the ground. There, in the wet sand, lay a full set of clawed footprints. The prints were larger than those they had seen earlier and pointed in the direction they were going. Even as they watched, water began to seep into the prints.

"It must be right ahead of us," Daniel said hoarsely as he stared into the darkness.

"It will see our light," said Lydia, clutching Daniel's arm.

"It will eat us!" cried Max. "I want to go home!"

"Be still," snapped Daniel. "It will eat us if you two keep screeching. We have to keep going. Don't you see, this river has to come out somewhere, maybe outdoors. Walk slower. Maybe the monster will move far ahead of us. Lydia, you carry the food and the egg. Max, you carry the torch."

"Then what will you carry?" asked Lydia,

tying the food sack's leather thong to her waist in order to free her arms.

"I won't carry anything," Daniel answered patiently, wiping the water from his face. "But I'll go first and my body will shield the light of the torch. If we're lucky, there will still be enough light for me to see by."

"All right," said Lydia. "But be careful."

They rearranged their burdens and began walking cautiously, peering in all directions. The sand grew wetter and more unstable. Moisture shimmered in the air, plastering their hair against their heads and saturating their clothes. Each step seemed more difficult than the last.

"Look," said Daniel, pointing ahead. "The river is turning. See, it curves off to the right."

"It's spreading out," said Lydia. "It looks calmer."

As they approached the bend, it seemed that Lydia was right. The river widened and flowed more smoothly, and to their amazement it was warm to the touch.

"Let's cross to the other side," said Daniel. "Then we'll be even farther away from the monster. Hold tight to the person in front of you."

Sliding one foot in front of the other,

Daniel entered the river, pulling Max, then Lydia after him.

"Be careful," he called over his shoulder. "The current is still strong!"

They were in midstream and the water was lapping at Max's waist when the torch began to flicker.

"Oh, no," whispered Lydia. "Please, Gods, make the light stay on." But in spite of her prayers, the torch continued to dim. She clung to Max's sodden jerkin and held the precious egg more tightly.

Suddenly the darkness was shattered by a bellow so loud their eardrums ached. Eyes wide with terror, Lydia saw a huge head with tiny eyes and a great gaping mouth filled with jagged teeth rising out of the water and coming straight at them. Max's screams echoed her own, and stumbling backward, he dropped the torch. Instantly they were swallowed by the dark. Lydia screamed again, already sensing the grip of jagged teeth.

"Run!" she cried. Turning to her left, she stumbled in the same direction as the current, pulling her brothers behind her. Daniel and Max cried out, but their words were lost as the monster uttered another awful roar.

Fear replaced caution and Lydia plunged forward. She had taken no more than four paces when her feet were swept out from under her. Her hand was wrenched free of Max's jerkin and she fell into the water, carrying the egg with her. She opened her mouth to scream, but water poured in and she could do no more than gasp and splutter. She tried to stand but the depth and the speed of the water had increased.

"Help! Help!" she cried, clinging to the egg in desperation, but there was no answer. She fought the current, which grew stronger and stronger. Then, as her strength began to flag, the bottom dropped away, leaving her no support at all except for the egg, which continued to float.

Lydia twisted her hands around the dragonskin that held the egg, determined not to let go as she was swept along by the torrent.

May the Gods protect me, she thought as she felt herself swept up and then hurtled down into nothingness.

15

At the Forge

Iestyn collapsed against the doors of his workshop and lay there pale and still. Not even the cries of his wife and son were able to pierce the black cloud of his unconsciousness. Toward morning, as the cold dirt floor spread an aching chill through his body, he wakened with a sudden rush of fear.

The urgency that had driven him so mercilessly during his trip down the mountain had deserted him, and it took several attempts before he was able to stand. Staggering on numbed feet, he pulled himself into the hay-filled wagon. He uncovered the black egg with trembling hands and examined it carefully. Only when he was certain that it was safe and whole did he descend.

Limping to the forge, he mounded it high

with charcoal. Then he lit the fuel with a firestone and fanned it with the great leather bellows. Lifting his left hand, he peered at it between swollen eyelids and cursed it for the stiff, unbending claw it had become. Angrily he swept everything from his workbench and heaped a great pile of hay on its surface. Then he fashioned a large nest and lined it with a soft leather cloth used for polishing metal.

Satisfied with his handiwork, he carefully lifted the egg down from the wagon and placed it in the nest. He fanned the fire higher and higher until heat waves shimmered in the air and sweat poured from his brow. "Got to keep it warm," he mumbled, and allowing the bellows to swing free, he reached for a pile of pelts that he had once taken in trade.

The egg sat black and majestic on its crude nest as Iestyn carefully covered it with the thick furs. Then he collapsed on the low bench that stood next to the worktable and stared at the prize for which he had risked so much.

What if it's too warm? he worried. How do I know when it's warm enough? A chicken, he thought, fighting off the red haze that threatened to engulf his mind. Maybe a chicken would know.

Ignoring his body's protests, he pushed

himself to his feet and staggered through the door that connected the forge with the barn. He caught a startled chicken that had been brooding on its nest and, clutching it to his chest, returned to the forge.

"A chicken will know," he muttered. "Even if the egg is big, it's still an egg." Tossing the pelts aside, he placed the frightened chicken atop the enormous egg. It cackled hysterically and flapped away, coming to rest on a pile of metal rods.

"Get back here, you stupid bird, or I'll wring your scrawny neck!" he snarled as he lunged for the bird. Twice more he caught it and twice more it escaped. After the next capture, both bird and man were exhausted and the chicken remained where it was placed.

Panting, the chicken rolled its eyes, then settled down atop the giant egg with an air of resignation. "There," said Iestyn with satisfaction as he sat down on his bench, "that should help."

Then, almost against his will, his eyes began to close. He blinked them open and tried to stay awake, but his injured body was claiming its dues. Abandoning all resistance, he sprawled on the bench and slept.

Perhaps the dreams were caused by the pain, but as Iestyn slept he dreamed that he was lost in an unknown place, surrounded by darkness and thick red mist. He knew with certainty that the mists concealed something he had yearned for all his lonely life. He plunged through the mists, trying to find the elusive prize, but always, just as he drew near, it disappeared, never even granting him a glimpse of its form.

Again and again, a man appeared out of the gloom. He was fair of face and perfect in every way and with his presence he held back the darkness.

But time and again a small, ugly dark man rose up out of the shadows and struck a killing blow. And as the fair man died, the darkness returned, bringing with it an overwhelming sense of evil.

Iestyn's mind whirled in torment. Goodness and grief battled pride and pain and there was no winner.

Throughout the days that followed, there were brief periods of wakefulness and sanity when Iestyn tended to the fire and the chicken and choked down a few handfuls of dry corn and raw eggs. At those times, it seemed to him that the egg was controlling him, forcing him to care for it and carry out its will. "Don't be daft," he muttered. "It's only an egg. How could an egg make me do anything? I know what I'm doing and I'm doing this because I want to. I'm going to be king of the world."

Then his weakened body would fail and he would sink into the mists where his soul continued to fight for its existence.

His wife and son came often to the great barred doors but, fearing his terrible wrath, dared not speak. Occasionally they heard him talking to himself and felt the heat of the forge and reasoned that all was well. They placed bowls of food within the barn, next to the supply of charcoal, and never knew that it was cats who ate their offerings.

Iestyn's torment continued, and as he grew weaker it seemed to him that the black egg pulsed with power, radiating a promise of what was yet to come.

16

The Underground City

It seemed to Lydia that she fell through the warm torrent of water for a very long time, but in truth, it could scarcely have been more than a few moments. As she fell, a great calmness came over her. By the Gods, if I get out of this alive, she thought, I promise I'll be nicer to Daniel.

The water swept her down and she held the egg even more tightly as she plunged into the fury that lay at the foot of the waterfall.

Once, twice, three times, she surfaced and was beaten under by the force of the water. Fighting the panic that threatened to overwhelm her, she took one deep breath and then allowed the deluge to thrust her far below the surface. Once free of the conflict, she swam underwater, towing the bulky dragonskin bundle behind her. Finally she was able to escape the pull of the river. Coughing and choking, she waded into shallow water and fell on the bank.

Dimly, as though from a great distance, she realized that there was light. She tried to stand, but could not; her heavy, waterlogged skirts and shaky legs held her down. Pushing the egg before her, rejoicing in its safety, she crawled out onto the warm sand of the riverbank and collapsed.

It seemed no time at all before someone shook her rudely, calling her name and forcing her back to consciousness.

"Go away," she said irritably. "I'm tired."

"Thank the Gods! She's alive!" said a voice filled with relief. And slowly she became aware of Max crying.

"Why are you crying?" she asked, pushing herself into a sitting position.

"'Cause you were dead," sniffled Max, wiping his nose with the back of his hand.

"Don't do that!" snapped Lydia, fumbling in her pocket for a soggy handkerchief. "I've told you a hundred times to use your handkerchief."

"I guess you're not dead," said Max, smiling through his tears. "You can't yell if you're dead."

"I was just sleeping," said Lydia. "And I

wasn't yelling. What happened to you two? How did you get away from that monster?"

Then she noticed her surroundings for the first time and gaped in amazement. Huge multistoried dwellings climbed the walls of the cave on both sides of the river. "Where are we?" she asked.

"Unbelievable, isn't it? A whole city built into the sides of the cliffs and all underground," replied Daniel.

"Does anyone live there?"

"I don't know," said Daniel. "We only found you a few minutes ago. You know almost as much about it as we do. But I don't see any sign of people. It looks deserted."

"How did you get here? What happened?"

"Well," said Daniel as he unwrapped the dragonskin and checked the egg carefully, "you distracted the monster just long enough for us to escape. I grabbed Max and swam for the other side. I bumped into a rock overhang and we hid under it until we heard the monster leave."

"Then we followed the river until it went over the edge of this real high cliff!" exclaimed Max. "The light came back and we climbed down. Did you go down the waterfall?"

"Of course she did. How else do you think

she got here?" said Daniel. "It's a wonder she wasn't killed. But the egg is unharmed, so far as I can see."

"If you haven't noticed, the sand is warm here," said Lydia, pushing a wet strand of hair off her cheek. "In fact, this cave is much warmer than the last one. I hope it's keeping the egg at the right temperature."

Holding on to her brother's arm, Lydia stood shakily and looked around.

"Where does the light come from?" she asked.

"I think it's some kind of mineral," said Daniel. "See how it hangs in clusters on the walls and roof of the cavern? It works quite well."

"But that's not how we got down the waterfall cliff," Max said. "It was the bugs!"

"Bugs?" queried Lydia, turning a puzzled face to Daniel.

"The bugs from the first cave, Lydia. It was incredible! You should have seen them!" exclaimed Daniel. "Just as we came to the edge of the cliff, they flew over us in a giant cloud. There were so many of them, we had time to climb down before the last of them disappeared."

"But where were they going?" Lydia asked.

"I don't know, but I hope they were going outside. Maybe they leave the cavern each night and return at dawn," said Daniel. "That would mean we have a chance of getting out of here. Maybe we can follow them!"

"I think it's a great idea!" said Lydia. "You were sure lucky that they flew over when they did."

"We probably wouldn't have found our way down if they hadn't," admitted Daniel.

"You could have swum," Lydia said with a grin. "It was very exciting."

"I don't know how you did it," Daniel said admiringly. "I would have died of fright."

"I almost did," admitted Lydia, and they smiled at each other, sharing a moment of friendship.

"Come on!" Max cried impatiently. "Are you going to talk forever? Let's explore."

The sand remained warm as they walked toward the cliff dwellings on the remains of smooth stone paths.

"Are you sure no one lives here now?" asked Lydia in a small voice.

"I don't think so," said Daniel as he looked up at the hundreds of dark windows that stared down at him. "But maybe . . ."

"Look at what I found!" cried Max, who had been poking in the sand a few paces ahead. He ran to meet them and placed a clump of glowing rock crystals in Daniel's hand. "It looks like rock candy," he said.

"So it does," said Daniel, examining the glowing crystals, "but I'm afraid you can't eat it."

"I'm hungry," said Max.

"You're always hungry," said Lydia. She examined the contents of the sack that still hung at her waist. "Well, the bread's all wet, but we've still got some cheese and a little bit of meat."

"Why don't we see if we can find a way up into the houses before we eat?" said Daniel. "I don't know if there are any monsters around, but I'd feel safer if we were out of their reach."

"Maybe we shouldn't go up there," said Lydia with a shiver. "I feel like someone's watching me."

"It's only your imagination," said Daniel. "But I'm not even sure we *can* get up there."

"We could climb up," said Max.

"Oh, sure," said Lydia. "How?"

"The same way we climbed down the waterfall," said Max. He pointed to the face of the cliff. "On those steps." And there, carved into the soft golden sandstone, was a set of deeply grooved hand- and footholds.

It took them a long time to climb to the first level, burdened as they were by the egg and the food sack, which seemed to grow heavier at every step. And as they clung to the narrow grooves, they realized that the

wall curved outward to form a rock overhang. Only with difficulty and great care
were they able to pull themselves up onto a
narrow rock ledge and through a round
doorway cut in the rock.

"Look at this place!" gasped Daniel as he
lay sprawled upon the rough rock. "One
person could hold off an army on this ledge.
It would be impossible to sneak past."

"I can see why," said Lydia. "I'm half
dead from the climb alone."

"Let's see what we can find," said Daniel.
He stood up, cradling the egg in his arms.

The entry room, the only one that actually
opened onto the ledge, was empty except for
a few broken spear points and pieces of clay
pots. A long string of rooms opened, one
after the other, beyond the first one. Each
had been carved out of the glittering sandstone and had suffered little from the passage
of time. Every room had narrow window
slits that gave a clear view of the river.
Niches were carved in the walls, but held no
household gods; instead, most held chunks of
the glowing crystals, which shed a soft warm
light. There were numerous tall spaces
carved in the walls which bore the imprint of
spears.

"Maybe they had a war or something and
they all died," said Daniel.

"Let's see what's on the next level," urged

Lydia. "I keep thinking someone's watching me and it gives me the shivers." Without waiting, she climbed a set of grooves that led up through a hole to the next floor. "Come on up," she called down. "This is where they lived. It's much nicer."

Slinging the dragonskin bundle over his shoulder, Daniel climbed up with Max at his heels.

The view from the wide arched windows on the second level was breathtaking. As the children perched on the broad sills, they could see the waterfall where they had been and the immense river canyon where they had yet to go.

They explored the empty rooms, scuffing their way through the dust which lay thick on the floor and making many discoveries. In one room they found a firestone, and in another a scattering of painted clay pots. Max found a room that held brightly colored murals. They showed people much like themselves, clad in curious robes of an ancient design and staring out at the children as though they were intruders. But it was Lydia who made the two greatest finds.

"Come quickly," she called, her voice rising in excitement. Her brothers raced to her side. "Look," she said, pointing to a large clay jar that stood in a dark corner. "It's got pictures of corn painted on it. Maybe there's corn inside!"

"Lydia, how would corn grow under a mountain?" asked Daniel. "And even if it could, this place has been abandoned for a long time. Whatever was inside that jar has turned to dust long ago."

"Maybe not," replied Lydia. "Look, the jar is sealed with an oiled hide and tied with leather thongs just like Granny Roone does it. If I'm right, there's a layer of wax under the hide. Granny says that doing things the old way will keep food fresh till doomsday." Picking at the stiff thongs with nervous fingers, she freed them and peeled back the hide.

"Well!" she exclaimed. "There's no corn—but there's dried mushrooms!"

"Oh, yuck," said Max.

Lydia picked up a mushroom and studied it. "Seems all right," she said. "It's a kind that Granny Roone gathers. If we're lucky, we'll find more jars with different things to eat." But no more jars were found.

As though to make up for her disappointment, the next room contained a stone face carved high on the wall. Water, clear and cold, flowed through its mouth and fell in a shimmering stream into a beautifully carved catch basin, which emptied through a small hole in the bottom. In the far corner was another pool carved in the stone floor. It bubbled and steamed, sending waves of warmth into the room. The rear wall held another of the bright murals, which was lit by a softly glowing rock perched in a high niche.

"This is it," said Daniel as he wearily lowered the egg to the floor. "We'll eat and sleep here. It's warm and dry, and we're too high for the monsters to get us. We can think about leaving after we've had some sleep."

"Agreed," said Lydia.

The children relaxed for the first time since they left the dragon's lair. After a frugal meal, they arranged themselves around the egg and finally slept.

17

The Secret Panel

"Daniel, wake up! Where's the egg? Did you put it somewhere?" cried Lydia as she shook her brother roughly.

"Wha—?" Daniel replied, bleary with sleep.

"Oh, wake up! The egg! The mushrooms! They're gone!" Lydia cried in frustration. "Tell me if you moved them!"

"The egg?" Daniel said groggily. "What's wrong with the egg? Is it hatching?"

"How should I know, you dolt, it's gone!" shrieked Lydia. "Open your eyes!"

Daniel shook his head and blinked his eyes wide. "The egg! It's gone!" he exclaimed in amazement. "Where's it gone to?"

"You dummy! That's just what I've been saying. The egg is gone! I knew we were being watched! I felt it! We're not alone here and someone has stolen our egg. We've got to get it back!" Lydia raged.

"Max, wake up! Someone's stolen the egg," said Daniel as he gently shook his brother's shoulder. "I'm afraid they took your bear bowl too."

"Hurry up!" cried Lydia. "We've got to find that egg. What if the thief eats it?"

"It's behind that wall," Max said sleepily. He pointed at the wall with the mural.

"Oh, Max, get up and help us look," said Lydia.

"I'm not making it up. The egg's behind that wall," said Max.

"Max, it's a solid wall," Lydia said in an annoyed tone. "If you want to stay here, fine, but I'm going to look in the other rooms."

Leaving Max sitting next to the painted wall, Daniel and Lydia searched all the rooms on the second level, but found no sign of the egg or the thief.

"This is terrible," said Daniel as they returned to the room where they had camped. "We've got to find that egg."

"It's behind this wall. I know it is," said Max.

"Why do you say that, Maxie?" asked Daniel.

"I just know," said Max, looking at his feet. "I can feel it."

"I'm not going to listen to this nonsense," Lydia said angrily. "I'm going to keep looking," and turning on her heel, she left the room.

"Daniel, you believe me, don't you?" asked Max.

"Oh, Max, I don't know what to think," answered Daniel. "And I don't know what to do," he added, tears filling his eyes. "I wish I did. Lydia always seems to know what to do. Even when she's wrong she pretends she's right. I keep thinking of what Father would do and how he would expect me to act. But I'm not Father. How can I make everything be all right when I don't know how?"

"It will be all right, Daniel," said Max. "I know it will."

"Thanks, Maxie," said Daniel, wiping his eyes with the back of his sleeve. Then, laughing shakily, he said, "Uh-oh, I better not let Lydia see me, or she'll yell at me for not using a handkerchief. Come on, let's take a look at this wall."

They searched the wall, aided by the light of the glowing crystal clump up in its niche. The people in the painting seemed to watch them, their eyes full of secret humor. But the boys found nothing.

Lydia returned and the three children gathered by the spring, tired, hungry and covered with dust.

"There's got to be a secret passage some-where," Lydia said with a sigh. "It's the only answer. But I just can't find it."

"It's behind this wall," Max said stub-bornly.

"Max, we looked," Daniel said patiently. "We looked at every inch of that wall and didn't find a thing."

"It's there," Max insisted again. "I just know it is."

"There are still two more levels that we haven't searched," said Lydia. "Maybe the egg is up there."

"I'm going to take another look around," said Daniel. "You two stay here."

"I'm coming too," said Lydia, getting to her feet.

"No, you stay here with Max. I don't want him here by himself," said Daniel.

"You can't tell me what to do!" said Lydia, but she did not follow as Daniel left the room.

"You shouldn't be so mean to him," said Max as Daniel's footsteps faded away.

"Oh, Max, I try to be nice to him. It's just that he makes me so angry."

"You should try harder. How come you

blame him every time something goes wrong?"

"I don't either!" said Lydia.

"You do so," said Max. "And you say things that hurt."

"I don't mean them!"

"Then you shouldn't say them," said Max. "I don't like it when you call me a baby. And Daniel doesn't like it when you say he's a dummy. You shouldn't call people names, they won't like you."

"That just proves you're a dumb baby," Lydia said. "I have lots of friends."

"No, you don't," said Max. "Your friends are all afraid of you. I heard Vanda talking to Janine. Vanda said you're bossy and mean. And Janine said her father made her be friends, 'cause Father was the Dragonlord."

"Why didn't anyone ever tell me?" Lydia said in dismay.

"'Cause you'd have punched them," said Max. "But Daniel and I are your family, and you should be nice to us. We like you even if you are mean sometimes."

"Oh, Max, I never realized . . ." said Lydia in a stricken voice. "I don't mean to be awful. I'll try harder. I promise!"

Max watched his sister warily. To his amazement, he saw that there were tears in her brown eyes.

When Daniel returned some time later, he found them sitting with their backs against the wall, talking quietly.

"I couldn't find anything," he said dejectedly.

"I've been thinking," said Lydia. "If Max is so sure the egg's behind this wall, then maybe we should explore this room and the next one for a secret passage."

"I already did that," said Daniel as he lay down on the floor and stared glumly at the ceiling. "I couldn't find anything."

"That doesn't mean it's not there," Lydia said calmly. "It just means you didn't find it. Come on, Daniel, let's look again."

"All right," Daniel said wearily. Crawling to his feet, he allowed Lydia to pull him toward the wall. "Everyone stay behind me. If we do find something, I don't want either of you getting hurt."

"I've got my knife," said Lydia.

"And I can hit them with a . . . with a"— Max looked around—"with a rock!" He jumped up and grabbed the glowing crystal from its niche in the wall. As he did so, a section of the painted wall swung open, revealing a dark passage beyond.

"*Oh!*" gasped Max, his eyes growing large with surprise.

"You did it, Max! You found the secret

passage!" said Daniel. "This is what we've been looking for."

Holding the glowing crystal before them, they eased through the open panel and found themselves in a narrow passage that paralleled the rooms on the second level. Tiny cracks in the walls provided places where one could spy in on the rooms.

"That's how they watched us," whispered Daniel. "They knew what we were doing all the time. Hide that light, Max. Both of you stick close to me and be very, very quiet. If they're in here I don't want them to hear us coming."

Using the cracks of light as a guide, Daniel turned left and walked slowly down the dark corridor with his sword drawn and his ears alert for the smallest sound.

"Daniel, do you hear it?" whispered Lydia. "It sounds like somebody singing."

"I hear it," said Daniel, and they moved more swiftly, drawn by the eerie crooning that seeped down the corridor.

"What is it?" whispered Lydia, gripping her knife tighter. The strange, tuneless melody quavered up and down without pattern or rhythm. "It's scary."

"I don't know," said Daniel. "It sounds kind of like the way the Holy Ones sing at home on High Holy Days."

"Daniel," gasped Lydia softly. "Maybe it's a secret religion! Maybe they're sacrificing our egg!"

"You could be right," whispered Daniel. "That would explain why they stole it! Come on, we've got to stop them!" And holding his sword before him, Daniel raced down the corridor toward the sound of singing.

Lydia and Max were close behind, determined not to be left. The crystal showed a sharp turn to the right and another to the left. The singing grew louder and the darkness began to fade. Suddenly the children turned another corner and plunged into the middle of a room and came to an abrupt halt.

A fire roared in the middle of the room. Beyond it, on a low stone altar, sat the blue egg, the bear bowl and a long, curved sword. And right in front of the altar, sitting cross-legged in the sand, was the oldest man the children had ever seen.

18

The Last Survivor

The little old man sat facing the altar, bowed as if in worship. Long white hair flowed around his shoulders. But he wasn't dressed in robes like a Holy One—his scrawny body was naked except for a small scrap of hide that hung from his bony hips.

Startled by the sound of the children's entry, he turned his head toward them. A terrified expression crossed his wrinkled face. Stumbling to his feet, he snatched the sword from the altar. Lydia ran forward with her knife raised high.

"No, wait!" shouted Daniel as he grabbed her by the wrist. "Stop!"

The little man faltered. The heavy sword wavered, then snicked through the air and buried its point in the soft sand.

"Keep still," Daniel hissed at Lydia.

"Let me go! He's going to kill our egg!" she cried, struggling against her brother's grip.

"Kill the egg?" queried the old man in a shaky voice. "Thee thought I would kill the Unborn One? Nay, I would not see it brought to harm."

"Then how come you stole it from us? And how come you took our food and how come you're hiding in here?" spat Lydia.

"And you took my bear bowl too," added Max.

"Why, the egg is mine," the old man said in astonishment. "I have prayed for many sleeps and the Gods have answered by sending the Unborn One to me. It is a reward for my long vigil."

"I don't think we understand what you're saying," said Daniel as he thrust Lydia behind him. "Why don't we all put our weapons in that corner and sit down and discuss this calmly."

"Thee speaks with a wisdom beyond thy years," said the old man, and tugging the massive curved sword by its handle, he dragged it to the far corner.

Then, as he sank cross-legged before the altar, Daniel, Lydia and Max laid down their own weapons.

"I think he's lying," whispered Lydia as

they arranged themselves on the soft sand.

"I hope you're wrong," murmured Daniel. "But I think we should at least talk to him. He doesn't look dangerous. You weigh more than he does.

"We pray thee, sir, tell us thy name and how thee come to be here," said Daniel, struggling to remember the formal style of speech that the Holy Ones used at home in the temple. "Tell us thy story and we shall do the same."

"There is not much to tell and there has not been another to tell it to for many, many sleeps," said the old man. "For I, Tyrus, am the last of The People."

"What people?" Lydia asked suspiciously.

"THE People," answered Tyrus with great dignity.

"Why are you the last of your people?" Daniel asked. "What happened to them?"

"They died," Tyrus said simply. "I am the last of The People and when I pass, we will be no more."

"Maybe you should tell us this story from the beginning," said Daniel. "Where did your people come from? How come you live underground?"

"In the beginning there were The People and The Others," Tyrus said in a singsong voice. "And time was divided by brightness and darkness. Fire Lords flew overhead and all gave homage to them. Then The Others rose up and killed the Fire Lords and warred upon The People, and The People fled until they came to a place of safety where The Others would not follow. There was no brightness and The People wandered in darkness and fear. Then they discovered the City of Light and made it their own. The Others were afraid to follow and there was a time of peace. The People lived in the City for many lifetimes and learned to glean the fish from the river and the plants from the sands. But some were sad and yearned for the life of old. They braved the beasts of darkness and searched the far reaches of this world.

"They returned with tales of another land where light and dark lived in harmony. A land where The People could live in safety from The Others. But the land was guarded by a Fire Lord who ate all who entered. There was hunger in the City and many chose to leave. They swore to tame the Fire Lord or die in the trying. They never returned.

"Others, my ancestors among them, did not believe there was a world beyond the Caves. They chose to stay. Their wisdom saved The People."

"But that's crazy," Lydia said. "How could they know there was no other world?"

"There is no other world beyond the Caves," Tyrus said firmly. "There is only darkness. I know this to be true, for once I climbed to the top of the falling water and traveled to the place where the river begins, and there was only darkness. It was the end of the world."

"No, Tyrus, not the end of the world," Daniel said quietly. "Nor was it the outside where both light and dark are found. It was just another cave. The outside lies far beyond the cave where the river begins."

"There was no light. It was the end of the world," Tyrus said stubbornly.

"Weren't the lightbugs there?" asked Max.

"No, they flew past me as I traveled," said Tyrus. "They do so twice each sleeptime."

"We think they go outside every night," said Daniel. "You were going the wrong way. You should have followed them. They would have led you outside."

Tyrus frowned. "No, it cannot be. That way lies danger. There is no world beyond the Caves."

"Then where do you think that jar came from?" demanded Lydia, pointing to the jar of mushrooms in the corner. "Those are pictures of corn on it, and corn doesn't grow in caves. Your ancestors must have brought that jar into the mountain with them."

"I do not know this corn," said Tyrus

without interest. "The jar is painted with sacred symbols of the ancients. It has always been here. There is nowhere else."

"If there is no other world, then what happened to your people when they left here?" asked Lydia.

"The darkness ate them," Tyrus said with certainty. "They should never have left."

"What happened to the people who stayed?" asked Daniel. "Where are they?"

"When the others left there were not enough spears to hold back the Hotas. They grew more bold and feared us less. They trod our gardens and tore our nets. Many fell to the Hotas' teeth and never warmed our sands again."

"What are Hotas?" asked Max.

"Hotas?" Tyrus exclaimed in astonishment. "How can thee come from the Gods and not know about the Evil Ones!"

"We don't come from the Gods," said Lydia. "We come from Gallardia and there aren't any Hotas there."

"I think he means the monsters," said Daniel. Smoothing the sand, he drew an outline of the river monster.

"Hota!" cried Tyrus, throwing up his arms and cringing in fear.

"Calm thyself," said Daniel, wiping the sand smooth. "It is only a drawing. I did not mean to frighten thee."

"They will come if thee summon them," whispered Tyrus. Scrambling to his feet, he hurried to the fire and spat into it three times. Then he quickly bowed to the household god that sat in a niche on the wall. "Perhaps they did not hear."

"You don't really believe that, do you?" scoffed Lydia.

"Of course," said Tyrus. "How can thee not believe in them? They are real."

"I give up," said Lydia. "We could talk forever and he'd never understand."

"Tyrus, we do not come from the Gods, but we have been charged with an important task which we must complete," Daniel said quietly. "To finish this task, we must find our way out of these caves and take our egg with us. Will you help us?"

"No," Tyrus said firmly. "Thee have been sent by the Gods. I know this to be true. They have sent thee to me bringing the precious egg. And when I die it will carry my soul to them. I am thy mission and I will not let the egg go, ever."

"But I don't want to stay here," whimpered Max.

"I am sorry, little brother, but I did not ask thee to come. Thee were sent by the Gods."

19

A Change of Heart

None of the children's arguments convinced Tyrus that there was another world outside the caves. He soon grew tired of arguing and began to prepare a stew of fern stems, mushrooms and fish over a bed of glowing firestones. After serving the children, he left them to sleep before the waning fire, promising to return when they had wakened.

The children tried to settle down under the smiling gaze of Tyrus's household god, which though carved of stone instead of wood was much like the household gods at home. But they were too restless to sleep. Now that they had found the precious egg, the children were anxious to leave.

"Why don't we just punch him, take the egg and run?" asked Lydia as the three of them lay on the fire-warmed sand. "We know how to get out of here now. Why do we need him?"

"Because he has all the food," answered Daniel. "And it would be difficult to run carrying the egg. He knows this world better than we do. And besides, it wouldn't be right, leaving him here all alone. How would you like it?"

"I wouldn't like it," answered Max.

"But he won't come, Daniel," reasoned Lydia. "He doesn't think we're real. He couldn't even understand why we had to eat or sleep, since we were sent by the Gods."

"Then we'll just have to convince him to come," said Daniel.

"I wish we *were* Gods," Lydia said glumly as she stared into the fire. "Then we could command him to take us out of here."

"Lydia!" Daniel said excitedly. "That's it! That's perfect! That's just what we'll do! How clever of you to think of it!"

"Oh, don't be so dumb," Lydia said irritably, pleased in spite of herself with the unaccustomed praise. "It's not such a great idea."

"Yes, it is," said Daniel as he rolled over and looked at his sister. "You always have lots of good ideas. And they come to you so easily. I used to wish I was you."

"Really?" Lydia said in amazement. "I've always wished I were more like you! If I'd been more like you, Father would have liked me better."

"Lydia, that's not true," said Daniel. "Father loved you the way you are. He used to smile and say, 'What a wildcat, your sister.' He was proud of you."

"But he loved you boys best," insisted Lydia. "He was always hugging and snuggling Max."

"I asked him once if he loved me best," Max said with a faraway look in his eyes, "and he said he loved us all best."

"I miss him," Lydia said brokenly. Tears began to trickle down her cheeks. "I wish I'd told him how much I loved him. I wish I'd let him snuggle me more."

"I miss him too," said Daniel, and soon all three children were crying.

The sound of their sobs brought the old man. He entered the chamber quietly.

"How can this be?" he asked in wonder as he touched their tears with his fingertips. "Gods do not cry."

"We're not Gods," wept Lydia. "We've told you and told you, but you won't listen. We're just children, ordinary everyday children."

"In truth?" the old man said. "Thee were not sent by the Gods?"

"No," wailed Max. "And we don't want to stay here anymore. I want my Granny."

The old man sank to the sand, and tears began to wander down his wrinkled cheeks. "I thought they had answered my prayers," he whispered. "Maybe the Gods are dead along with my people. And when I die there will be none to mourn me or sing the old songs and speed my soul on its way. Now I am truly alone."

"No, you're not," said Lydia, sniffling back her tears. "We're here. You have us."

Tyrus looked at Lydia and seemed to see her for the first time. A look of marvel filled his eyes. "If the Gods did not send thee, where did thee come from? And who are thee?"

"We tried to tell you before," said Daniel. "We're from Gallardia." And speaking all together and in turns, they told their story.

"It's true then?" Tyrus said in amazement. "The old stories are really true? There really is another world where the darkness eats the light? Do thee not fear for thy souls?"

"I don't like the dark," said Max, "but it never hurt my soul. At least I don't think so—I've never seen it."

Everyone laughed and Max blushed bright red.

"Tell me more about thy world," urged Tyrus. "It sounds a wondrous place."

"It's not just our world, Tyrus. It's your

world too and you could see it for yourself. All we have to do is follow the river," said Daniel.

"No," said the old man. "I could not leave. My place is here with my ancestors."

"Tyrus, please come with us," urged Lydia. "We need you to help us. We can't do it by ourselves."

"And besides, you don't want to stay here all alone," said Max. "It's scary and lonesome."

"Aye, it is that," agreed Tyrus. "But I am afraid. This world, even the Hotas, are known to me. Thy world would be new and hard."

"But you'd have friends," said Lydia. "We'd be there to help you. Please say you'll come with us."

"I will think on it," said the old man, and he left the children alone for a long while.

When he returned, an uncertain expression still on his face, Lydia asked encouragingly, "Have you decided? Will you be our friend and come with us?"

"Friend," said Tyrus, and his dim old eyes filled with tears. "I never thought to hear the word again. I have been alone so long. When I thought I was the only person left, there was nought I could do, but now, knowing thee exist, I could not bear the aloneness anymore. Maybe the Gods have sent thee to me as a message. Maybe they do not mean for me to end my life alone. Yes, yes, I will come!"

"I'm so glad!" said Lydia, and she flung her arms around the old man's neck and hugged him tight.

"Oh, er, um," humphed Tyrus. Hesitantly, he hugged her back. "It is many sleeps since I have felt another's touch," he said at last. "I am glad that thee are real."

"I'm glad too," said Lydia with a laugh. "Now, when can we go?"

"Soon," said Tyrus. "But I cannot just leave. I must say my farewells. Thee must be patient with this old man for yet a little while."

"Not too long," said Daniel. "There's not much food here and I want to be outside when the egg hatches."

"The life within is not yet ready to be born," said Tyrus. "There is time."

"What? How do you know that?" cried Daniel.

"I just know," the old man said with a shrug. He stepped over to the altar, where the egg still rested, and placed his hand against the shell. "I can feel the life beating within, sleeping deeply. It is not yet ready to waken."

"I knew that," said Max.

"Max, don't tell stories," said Daniel. "You promised not to fib."

"But I—"

"Thee must see the paintings of the Fire Lords," said Tyrus. "They are in the Burial Chamber."

Without waiting to see if they followed, Tyrus walked out the far side of the room, through another secret panel, down a long corridor and into an enormous room deep inside the cliff. Long, narrow cubicles lined the walls from floor to ceiling, and fragile skeletons, each accompanied by a tiny pile of personal possessions, filled the niches.

Bright murals covered what little space remained and showed vividly realistic pictures of dragons of every shape and color. Many clutched people in their claws. "The Fire Lords collect the souls and carry them to their rest," said Tyrus, gesturing toward the dragon paintings. "I thought that was why the egg had come."

"But Tyrus, you're not going to die yet," said Daniel. "You've got lots longer to live."

"Perhaps," said the old man as he led them back to the warm room where the blue egg sat. "Mayhap I will die when I reach this outer world. This could be but a jest of the Gods."

"Please don't worry, Tyrus," said Lydia.

"Everything will be all right. Tell me, is it far to the end of the river?"

"I do not know," answered Tyrus. "I have only been upriver. But the legends say that The People traveled long and there were many dangers along the way. They tell of Hotas and their evil cousins, the Pacibaras. And there are watersteps and places where the river flows in circles and swallows one whole."

"What are Pacibaras?" asked Daniel.

"They are creatures of the river," said Tyrus. "They are the color of death, and they lie in wait, watching for one foolish enough to enter their domain. Then they seize thee with their long wicked teeth and drag thee down to their lairs. There are many of them at the foot of our waterstep; they wait for the fish who are carried over the edge."

"Here? Outside here?" squeaked Lydia. "I was in that water for a long time!"

"Then thee were very lucky," said Tyrus, "for Pacibaras prefer the taste of man above all others."

"How big are they?" interrupted Daniel.

"They are the size of little brother when they are grown," said Tyrus. "But even the small ones are dangerous, for they will always attack."

"Well, we'll just stay out of the water then," said Daniel.

"That may not be possible," said Tyrus, "for I have fished the river as far as one may go and the path soon ends. Only the Gods know what awaits us."

"Then we'll build a raft," said Daniel. "I'm not getting eaten by Pacibaras."

"What is a raft?" asked Tyrus.

"It's a flat thing that floats. You build it out of wood," said Lydia.

"What is wood?" asked Tyrus.

"Oh, right. No wood inside mountains," said Lydia. "Any ideas, Daniel?"

"No," said Daniel. "I'll have to think about it."

"We will sleep now," said Tyrus, "and think later. Much has happened and even thee who are no longer Gods must sleep. Good rest to thee, young friends. I am glad that thee are here."

"Good rest," echoed the children, and comforted by hopes of escape, they slept deeply and well.

20

The
Hota
Boat

"I know what we're going to do," said Daniel as they ate bowls of hot fish stew. "It came to me as I slept."

"Ah, a vision," said Tyrus. "Sleep visions often solve problems that cannot be answered awake."

"What is it, Daniel?" asked Lydia.

"Well, I was thinking that if we had some oiled hides like the one on top of the mushroom jar, we could make big bags, blow them full of air and ride them down the river."

"Would it work?" asked Max as he pushed a mushroom aside and licked the last bit of fish from his bear bowl.

"I think so," said Daniel. "At least it did in

the dream. We were riding high in the water with Pacibaras all around us. They were snapping their teeth and having fits because they couldn't reach us. It was pretty funny."

"It is not wise to laugh at one's enemy," cautioned Tyrus. "The Gods have a strange humor. Often that which we mock becomes our destiny."

"I meant no disrespect," said Daniel. "It was only a dream. And since we don't have the hides and I wouldn't know how to make bags anyhow, it really doesn't matter."

"No, it is a good idea," said Tyrus. "And The People have used a device such as thee describe. The skins lie in the storeroom. When I have spoken to the Gods, I will get them for thee."

The children quickly finished the last of their stew and Tyrus bowed before the altar and egg, speaking silently to his Gods. Then they all filed into the room where the children had first slept and washed their bowls and fingers in the basin of hot water.

"How do you make this water hot?" asked Lydia. "I don't see any fire."

"It is a gift from the Gods," said Tyrus. "Its source is a sacred place. There is much heat and, if the Gods decree, sudden bursts of hot air that can kill thee with one breath."

"Tyrus! That's it!" Daniel exclaimed

loudly. "You must show me this place where the steam comes from. We can use it to fill the bags and make our escape."

"I will show thee if thee wish it," said Tyrus. "But I must make my offering to the Hota first."

"A Hota, here?" Lydia asked sharply.

"Of a sort," said Tyrus. He led them through a wall panel and into yet another corridor. "It is the skin of the Hota. We make it offerings in the hope that it will spare our flesh."

Suddenly Max let out a shrill scream and tried to run. But Tyrus grabbed his shoulder and said, "Stop, little brother. Its spirit no longer fills its body."

Max peeked out from behind Tyrus and peered up at the horrible creature that loomed above him. Twice the height of a man, the Hota stood on massive hindquarters with its smaller, clawed forepaws held before it. Tough gray scaly skin covered the body, from the tip of the great thick tail to the small triangular head. Mouth gaping, teeth glinting, eyes staring, the Hota seemed fully alive. On the ground lay some small bowls filled with a variety of dried foods.

"Whew, it sure looks real," Daniel said shakily. "How does it stay up? What's inside?"

"The flesh and bones were removed and it

was filled with the breath of the Gods," answered Tyrus.

"Now I know we're going to get out of here," Daniel said with a grin. "Tyrus, please take me to the source of this Gods' breath."

"The little ones must stay," said Tyrus. "It is not safe."

"I'm not a little one," blustered Lydia, but then, glancing at Max, she said, "Oh, all right. I guess someone has to stay with Max, but you better tell me everything when you get back."

"Promise," said Daniel, and he followed Tyrus down a ladder of grooves in the stone.

"Stay close to me, little brother," Tyrus said as they descended. "It is dangerous."

As they climbed lower, the air grew thick with steam and the walls were beaded with moisture.

"Step carefully," called Tyrus. "We are at the source."

Allowing Tyrus to guide him, Daniel stepped off the last foothold and found himself standing on a narrow ledge that skirted a large open pit. Far below, the center of the pit winked back at them, a fiery red-orange eye that heaved with constant motion.

"What is that?" asked Daniel, drawing back and shielding his face from the intense heat that rose out of the pit.

"Why, it is the Eye of the Gods!" Tyrus answered, glancing at Daniel in surprise. "Do thee not have such places in your world?"

"No," said Daniel. "I've never seen such a thing."

"Thine must be a very strange world," said Tyrus, shaking his head. Taking Daniel by the hand, he led him along the edge of the pit until they came to a place where the wall had split and torn itself open in some ancient violence.

Tyrus entered the crack, drawing Daniel behind him. The walls were deeply fissured and streaked with intense shades of red, yellow and orange, evidence of the stone's fiery past. Thin streamers of scalding steam hissed through the cracks. Daniel held his breath, trying not to inhale the fumes, which smelled of rotten eggs.

"It is safe to breathe," said Tyrus. "The Gods speak friendly words here. Their message grows more harsh as one goes deeper."

"I still don't understand how you fill the Hota," Daniel said. "You couldn't possibly bring it down here."

"It is not necessary to bring it down here," said Tyrus. "The Gods also speak through a small opening in the room where the Hota lives. All one must do is unstopper the tip of its tail and place it in the vent, and the Gods fill it with their breath."

"Why didn't you tell me that before?" demanded Daniel as he stared at the old man in frustration.

"Thee did not ask me!" Tyrus said indignantly. "Thee asked to see the source of the Gods' whisperings and that I have done!"

"That's true," Daniel said, vowing to watch his words more carefully in the future. "Well, now that I know, let's go back and tell the others."

The two retraced their steps carefully and soon rejoined Max and Lydia in the Hota's chamber. Daniel told what he had seen and outlined his plan for escape.

"Will it work?" Lydia said nervously. "Is it safe? I mean, it's so big. Do you really mean for us to climb on the back of that Hota and sail down the river? Will it float? What's to stop it from turning over and dumping us off? What if it snags on a rock and breaks? And even if it works, we'll look so stupid."

"One, I know it will float because Tyrus has taken very good care of it and it holds air fine. Two, it won't tip over because it's got sand in its feet to keep it weighted. Three, it won't snag because it's made out of Hota skin. Touch it. If those scales are tough enough to stop spear points, they can handle a few rocks, not to mention Pacibara teeth. And four, I don't care if we do look stupid. Who's going to see us except another Hota? And I'd rather look stupid than dead.

"But just in case anything does go wrong, we'll each have two oiled skin bags which I'll fill with the whispering air and tie together with thongs. If the Hota sinks or you fall off, the air bags will hold you up until you can be rescued. I'll even tie a set around the egg."

"What about the watersteps and that place Tyrus says swallows you?" asked Lydia.

"I don't know," said Daniel. "We'll just have to do our best and pray.

"Well, I think that's it. We'll have to make the skin bags and gather food, light crystals, spears and knives. Then we'll be ready to go. With any luck, we'll soon be safely out."

Their preparations took them several days, but at last everything was assembled on the sands at the edge of the river. The Hota bobbed gently in the current, tethered to the bank. They loaded their meager supplies and possessions aboard its scaly flanks and anchored them with the oiled skins inflated with hot air.

"Lydia, you take Max and sit in the middle. Tyrus will sit astride the neck and I'll be behind you," directed Daniel.

"Where will the egg be?" asked Max.

"Between Lydia and myself," answered Daniel. "She can help me hold it steady. And the hot air inside the sacks will help keep it warm."

"Let's go," said Lydia. "I'll be glad to see the last of this place."

"Not I," Tyrus said sadly, gazing upon the silent dwellings for the last time.

"But Tyrus, think of all the exciting things you're going to see," said Lydia. "You're going to like our world!"

"I have nought but thy presence and the old tales to say that such a place truly exists," Tyrus said. "I cannot imagine it."

"It's real, all right," said Daniel. "But we'll never see it unless we leave." He lifted Max and placed him on the broad back of the Hota and then climbed on board himself. Lydia stood on the sands, still eyeing the Hota boat with distrust, but she grasped Daniel's hand without comment and gingerly took her place in front of him and the egg.

Watched by the empty eyes of the abandoned buildings, Tyrus clasped his hands and bowed three times, bidding farewell to all he had known and loved. Then, turning abruptly, he pushed the Hota boat out of the shallows and leaped astride its massive neck.

The quick current swirled around the strange craft and nudged it into deeper

water. Then, with its snarling mouth pointing the way and its tail trailing behind, the
Hota boat slipped into the mainstream and
sailed majestically down the river, carrying
them toward their fate.

21

The Perilous Voyage

After all their preparations, it seemed for a time as though they might escape without trouble. The river ran smooth and calm and the movement of the Hota boat was soothing as it bobbed along on the swift current.

"This is fun!" cried Max. "Can we keep the Hota boat and do this again when we get home?"

"Can't you just see their faces, if we came sailing down the river on this at home?" Lydia said with a laugh. "Oh, Daniel, let's do it!"

"Lydia," Daniel said sternly, "you're not making any sense. If we get out of here alive, there will be a mountain between us and home. And we can't go back there anyhow or Iestyn will kill us."

"Hmmph," said Lydia. "If I were Dragon-lord, I wouldn't let that stop me."

"Look," said Tyrus, pointing to the shore where a high stone wall rose along the edge of the river. "That is where we had our gardens. Many things grew there but the Hotas desired them too and raided them from the river."

"We were wondering how you grew anything without sunlight," said Lydia.

"I do not know thy sunlight," said Tyrus, "but our crops always grew well by the light of the crystals. And even now, the wild mushrooms and ferns still grow here."

"Where do the Hotas live?" asked Daniel, hand on his sword. "Do they live around here?"

"They live in small groups," answered Tyrus. "Mothers travel with the young until they are old enough to care for themselves. The males wander alone, unless they are mating. Then they are filled with rage and will attack anything that moves. They are much to be feared at that time."

"I feared them before. I can't imagine them any worse," said Daniel.

"We caught a youngster once in our nets and tried to tame it," said Tyrus as he watched the sandy beach and the gold walls of the cave speed by. "But it never ceased trying to kill us and one day it escaped.

"Over there is a deep hole, ringed with stones to keep the Pacibaras out, where sometimes we swam. I remember one time—"

"Look!" shrilled Max, pointing ahead. "Something's coming! Look at the water. It's all whipped up!"

"Pacibaras!" cried Tyrus as they approached the frothing water. "Keep thy legs high!" When they drew level with the disturbance, he plunged his spear deep into the water. Seconds later a black stain roiled to the surface. There was a gnashing of teeth, and long black bodies, longer than Max and each the thickness of a strong man's arm, twisted and turned in the murky water. A narrow pointy head thrust itself out of the waves, its underslung jaw snapping and crunching a piece of its recent companion. A flat gray eye, devoid of intelligence, fixed them with a single hungry look and then sank below the waters.

"Pacibaras," Tyrus said again. "That is why thee must not fall off. Sometimes they go into a frenzy. Then even a Hota can be brought down."

"Don't worry," said Lydia, drawing her feet even higher up the flanks of the Hota boat. "I have no intention of falling off!"

"Good," said Tyrus. "This is the last of our land. I have traveled beyond this point only once, and that was many sleeps ago. Much may have changed since then."

Soon the strip of sand at the edge of the river narrowed, and the walls of the canyon drew closer. The roof of the cave, once distant, lowered, and the river was crested with short, choppy waves.

"What's happening?" asked Daniel as the Hota boat surged forward.

"This is the place I spoke of," said Tyrus. He opened a leather sack and took out a number of the glowing rocks.

"What place?" Lydia asked above the swelling noise of the river.

"It's another tunnel," said Daniel as Tyrus handed each of them a glowing rock, securely tied with a loop of leather.

"Will it be dark?" wailed Max.

"Hold thy tears, little brother," said Tyrus. He looped a thong over the ears of the Hota boat and centered an exceptionally large glowing rock on its forehead. "The Hota boat shall light our way and each of us will have his own light to hold back the darkness. Be brave."

"All right, I'll try," Max said in a small voice. "But I won't like it."

No sooner had he spoken than they were swept into a dark, narrow funnel of rough water. Sharp-edged rocks protruded from the river, threatening to puncture their craft.

Using the blunt end of their spears, Tyrus and Daniel guided the boat past them.

A chill wind whipped through their hair and the Hota boat sped forward at a dizzying speed. A sudden current wrenched them to the right and they slammed against the stone wall. Before they could draw a breath, the Hota boat was seized by yet another current and thrown back into the mainstream. Tyrus and Daniel fought to keep their craft centered and stable, but they lost control. The Hota boat and its passengers careened wildly from one side of the narrow channel to the other.

"Lie down!" Lydia screamed to Max. Wrapping her hands in the ropes of the air bags, she covered his trembling body with her own to shield him from as much of the violence as possible.

The walls drew closer. The river roared like a hundred Hotas as it plunged through the narrow space. The waves grew as high as the Hota boat's head, and the travelers were soon wet to the skin.

"Hold on!" yelled Tyrus. "I see watersteps ahead!"

The Hota boat shot over the edge of the first waterstep and landed heavily on the next. The current swung it sideways and it leaned ominously as it toppled over the ledge. Lydia screamed and cried, "Lean the other way or we'll capsize!" Daniel and Tyrus quickly obeyed and the Hota boat slowly righted itself, rolling from side to side as it regained its balance. Before they could settle themselves, they were swept onto a smaller series of watersteps that rattled their teeth and shook their limbs, and then were deposited harmlessly in a placid pool below the torrent.

"I wish there were some way to stop this thing," Daniel said in a shaky voice as the Hota boat sailed serenely on. He ran his hands over the various thongs and air bags. "The egg is still all right," he announced.

Now the river swept around a massive curve. As they rounded the bend, they saw that the water flowed into a dark opening in a solid rock wall.

Huge, jagged rocks lined the opening of this fearful entrance like teeth in a giant's mouth. The terrified travelers raised their legs as they were swept forward. Then they were there, and the Hota boat, too wide by far, jammed tight in the only opening between the rocks.

"We've got to get loose before the skin tears!" screamed Daniel.

They pushed and prodded the rocks with their hands and spears, attempting to free their craft. The water surged around them, building up behind the object that blocked the only route through, wedging the Hota boat tighter and tighter in the mouth of the water tunnel.

All at once there was a terrible hissing noise and the Hota boat shot forward, propelled by the force of the water behind it. The terrified passengers cried aloud, searching frantically for the torn place that would mean their death. But the Hota boat bounded on into the darkness of the tunnel, even as the hissing fizzled into silence.

"It was one of the air bags," said Tyrus in a voice weak with fear. "The Hota boat is whole. We are saved."

Before anyone could answer, a dull rumbling filled their ears, shaking the very air. Seconds later, the Hota boat reached the end of the water tunnel. By the dull glow of the light rocks, they saw that the water was now flowing sluggishly, swirling to their right. The Hota boat floated aimlessly until it too joined the circling.

"What's happening?" Max whimpered.

"This must be the Mouth of the Gods that the old legends speak of," said Tyrus. "I prayed that it was but a tale. But it is real. I fear we are doomed. We can only spin in circles until the God hungers and devours us. There is no escape."

Fearfully they gazed out over the water

toward the roaring center of the whirlpool, many yards away. Lighted by a yellow-green phosphorescence, it rose and fell, sucking down everything that entered the last and final circle.

"Dogsbreath!" snarled Lydia. "I'm not going to be swallowed by some stupid watercircle. Look, we're still on the far edge. The river continues over there on the other side. I bet if we paddled hard, we could break free. Come on, don't give up! Daniel, help me!"

"Yes, you're right," Daniel said with determination. Leaning over, the two of them began to paddle with their hands.

"It's hopeless," Tyrus said in despair. "It is the will of the Gods. Thee must say thy prayers."

"Paddle now and save thy prayers for later, old man!" yelled Daniel. "Help us!"

Reluctantly Tyrus bent over the side of the Hota boat and began scooping water away, saying his prayers all the while.

"Not that side!" screamed Daniel. "This side!"

As they paddled, Max uttered a terror-stricken cry. They looked up and saw an immense Pacibara, longer and thicker than a grown man, caught in the eye of the whirlpool. They watched its desperate struggles against the force of the water, saw the flash of an anguished eye. Then it was gone, swallowed whole by the great watery maw.

"Harder! Pull harder!" cried Daniel. They flailed the water, urging their craft outward with wild cries. Slowly, with agonizing efforts, they inched their way out of the deadly circle.

At last the maddening roar diminished and they floated free upon the black waters, drifting along on the smooth current.

"Oh," gasped Daniel as he stretched out on the hind flank of the Hota boat. "I'm so tired, I can hardly move."

Tyrus collapsed weakly against the neck of the Hota. Lydia slumped over Max, trying to catch her breath.

"I was so scared. I didn't think we'd make it," she said. "I think I could sleep for two moons."

"We will when we get out of here," said Daniel.

The Hota boat swept around another bend in the underground river. The glowing rock that dangled between its eyes lighted a stretch of stony ground that extended far into the water. There, standing on the edge of the spit, was a family of Hotas, one full-grown female and two young.

It was hard to say who were the more astonished, the Hotas or the humans. But as the humans gazed in startled terror at the Hotas, the fearsome creatures stared stupidly at the Hota boat sailing past them, carrying its human cargo.

Suddenly Daniel began to laugh. "Did . . . did you see the look on that Hota's face?" he said. "I thought its eyes would fall from its head."

"It is not wise to mock one's enemies," Tyrus said somberly. But soon he too was chuckling. The Hota boat floated on, wrapped in the laughter of those who had looked at death and escaped.

Their laughter turned to yawns and, exhausted by their efforts, one by one they slept. Daniel wrapped his hand in the thongs and held his spear at the ready, determined to keep watch. But the river swept on and its soft murmurings calmed him and lulled him to sleep.

He was wakened by a soft, delicate touch on his cheek. He smiled and opened his eyes. For one sleepy moment he thought himself at home with Granny Roone stroking his cheek. Then he saw the twinkle of stars and the glow of an orange moon. His eyes snapped open and he saw the long, slender branches of a water willow trailing over him.

He sat up slowly, feeling the cool, clean night air whispering past his face, full of the sweet, rich scents of black earth and growing things. The drone of small biting insects whined a welcome in his ears. The Hota boat rose and fell on the gentle current in the shallows where it had come to rest.

"Lydia, Max, Tyrus. Wake up. We're here. We made it," he said softly.

The others stirred slowly, rubbing their eyes with disbelief.

"Thee were right," Tyrus said, his voice thick with emotion. And Lydia turned to Daniel and clung to him without speaking.

The travelers dismounted stiffly from the Hota boat and waded the last few feet to the grassy bank. There they tied the Hota boat to the trunk of the giant willow. Then they carried the precious egg ashore and sat down to wait the coming of the dawn.

22

The
Black Egg

A fly sat on Iestyn's cheek and feasted on the ruin of his face. The soft movement somehow penetrated his numbed brain, which had ignored more persistent noises, such as Godfrey's knockings and demands that he answer.

He opened the one eye that would still respond and stared at the cracked and pitted surface of the table that lay in front of his face. Farther along lay an ugly thing, all twisted and black and useless. Dully, without feeling, Iestyn recognized it for what it was, his own left hand and arm.

Much of the pain had gone, or at least Iestyn no longer recognized it. His world had grown small, composed now of the black egg and whatever was necessary to serve it. Nothing else mattered, not even his own pain.

I must get up, he thought. I must see to the egg and the fire. But his weakened body refused to answer the commands of his brain and he continued to lie there, staring at nothing.

Then, suddenly, there was a deep wrenching twist inside his body and he bent nearly double with the agony of it. A terrible shock ripped through his skull and forced him to his feet. A great anxiety seized him and he knew with certainty that something was about to happen.

The chicken that had been perched high atop the black egg for so long clucked madly and flew away, roosting high in the rafters above the forge.

"It's happening!" exulted Iestyn. "It's hatching! My egg is hatching at last!"

A nameless compulsion drew him closer and closer until he knelt at the side of the enormous egg.

At first there was no outward sign that anything was occurring, but then he heard it, a small tapping from within the egg.

In the barn beyond the forge, the animals fell silent and stirred uneasily in their stalls. Birds sought their nests, and tucked their heads beneath their wings.

"It's happening!" cried Iestyn, and he hugged himself with joy.

The first thin crack did not appear for many hours, and long before then an incredible feeling, a curious mixture of excitement and joy, fear and loathing, had drawn people from the farthest reaches of the village to the forge, where they stood and waited for they knew not what.

"Why are we here?" asked Granny Roone, her face a map of sorrow. "I want nothing to do with the man. It's been almost a week since Godwin and the dragon and those others were found dead in the cave. And all that time Iestyn has hidden himself away in the forge. Why, I ask you? Because he's been up to no good. He's the one who killed Godwin and did away with my babies!"

"Hush, woman! You cannot prove it," muttered one of the Village Guard, who stood beside her. "There was no sign of his presence at the cave. The villainy belonged to the vermin who died there. You have no right to accuse the blacksmith."

"But why are we here?" asked the owner of the Dragon's Breath.

"I don't know," answered the guard. "I left my post to come. I didn't want to, but something kept pulling at me and here I am. I feel like something important is about to happen."

"And I was at my milking," replied another, "but I could do nothing but come. Do you think it's witchcraft? Are we under a spell?"

"I don't know," answered the guard. "I just knew that I must come. Whatever happens will find me here."

A murmur of assent followed his words, and the gathering, which grew larger with every passing minute, settled down to wait before the doors of the forge.

Within, the spider web of cracks pushed farther and farther across the egg, crackling and meshing with eerie precision. Iestyn watched, yearning to help, wanting only to seize his knife and tear away the shell, exposing the life inside. But something, some inner voice which spoke to him often lately, told him to wait. And he obeyed.

Outside the forge, the crowd grew larger. The Captain of the Guard came to break up the crowd, and stayed. The Palace Guard fared no better. Soon the forge was surrounded and most of the village, all but the king and the infirm, waited.

It was dusk before the first tiny hole appeared in the shiny black shell. It was only a pinprick but it grew rapidly, carved away by a scalpel-sharp ebony egg-tooth that sliced away the shell with surgical precision.

Following the inner voice, which had become a harsh command, Iestyn stumbled to his feet. As though in a dream, he saw himself build up the fire till it roared, heating the small building almost past the point of safety. His hair frizzed and crackled in the intense heat and his body shrank from the leaping fire, but the black egg glowed.

The hole was larger now and Iestyn held his breath as a small, slender snout emerged. The little mouth opened and tiny flames, each no larger than the flame of a candle, licked at the edge of the shell and crumbled it to ash.

Inside the egg, coiled like a tiny perfect puzzle, lay a small black dragon.

"My dragon," Iestyn whispered, and he reached out to touch it.

His hand was halfway to the egg when the dragon raised its head. Its tiny eyes glowed red in the firelight and fixed themselves on his, and a pain so fierce it could almost be seen tore through his body.

Iestyn felt the dragon's gaze growing stronger and stronger. The pain blasted him, unbearable in its intensity, yet he could not move.

Terror overwhelmed Iestyn as he struggled against the massive power that was sucking him dry, draining him of his very soul.

Then, just as suddenly as it had begun, the

pain ceased, and Iestyn felt something cold and black flow through him. His battered body stood tall and straight and arrogant. He was full of power and strength, and life surged strong in his veins.

He breathed deeply and threw back his head and laughed long and loud, because suddenly life was good.

"Come, little one, my black prince," crooned Iestyn, and reaching down he offered his twisted hand to the small creature.

Uncoiling in a single smooth motion, the dragon extended its head and neck. It seized Iestyn's hand with needle-sharp teeth and pulled itself free of the egg.

Dripping the fluids that had nourished and protected it for so long, it stretched first one black wing, then the other, to their full length, then rested as though exhausted by its small efforts.

"We must keep you warm, my little beauty," said Iestyn with a smile, heedless of the small, sharp claws that had fastened themselves to his arm. Moving closer to the fire, he fanned the flames higher and higher.

The little dragon stretched and twisted, absorbing the heat and drying its small, wet body. A flutter of motion caught its eye and craning its long neck it saw the hen that had brooded upon its egg. The chicken gave a small, helpless squawk, then flew silently down to perch alongside the dragon with dread in its eye. Beak agape, it stared in hopeless fascination.

The dragon struck, and in a few swift motions, the chicken ceased to exist, leaving only some white feathers to mark its passing.

For a time the dragon drowsed upon Iestyn's arm, enjoying the heat of the fire. Then, at last, it raised its little red eyes to Iestyn's and some unspoken message passed between them.

"Yes," said Iestyn. "It is time. We are ready."

He strode to the great double doors, threw back the bars that held them fast and flung them open.

They stood there in the doorway, the man and the dragon, lighted from behind by the roaring flames. Power and strength flowed from them and wrapped around the minds of all who observed them, and none could deny them.

Holding the black dragon on his arm, Iestyn walked forth among the crowd and knew that the world was his.

23

The Blue Egg

The dawn broke clear and cool and lay softly on the land. In time the sun rose over the snow-tipped mountain peaks, streaking the sky with crimson. Shortly after sunrise there was a brief shower, and when it passed, it left a rainbow for remembrance.

As the sun rose higher, warming the skies and the land, the rainbow faded and morning arrived with a rush. Birds sang, flowers nodded and jewel-bright butterflies flittered from leaf to leaf.

The great underground river poured forth from a hole in the base of the towering mountain. The Hota boat tugged at its tether, as though wishing to continue its journey.

"Thy world is so bright!" said Tyrus as he awakened and shielded his eyes with his hands.

"Yes, I suppose it is, after the caves," said Daniel. "But I think you'll get used to it."

"I will," the old man said with determination. "This is the world of my ancestors. To know that the old tales are true . . . I must see it!"

"You will," said Lydia. "Sit here in the shadow of the tree where it's not so bright. Maybe your eyes will feel better."

"What are thee going to do now? Thee will not leave me?"

"We wouldn't do that," said Daniel, "but I don't know what we're going to do next. I never had time to think this far ahead. All I thought about was getting out of there alive."

"Where are we?" Max asked sleepily from the warm cocoon of dragonskin which he shared with the egg.

"On the other side of the pass," Lydia said. "Somewhere in Bilbergia."

"I'm hungry," Max murmured. Then his eyes closed again and he fell asleep once more.

"I'm hungry too," said Daniel. "Let's look for some food. After that, we'd better try to figure out where we are. Maybe we can find a road and follow it to a town."

"But Bilbergia's our enemy!" cried Lydia. "We can't just give ourselves up!"

"Lydia, how are they going to know we're from Gallardia?" asked Daniel. "We're just three children out for a walk with our grandfather. We'll be safe enough till we can find someone to help us."

"But what about the egg?" asked Lydia. "What if it hatches before we find someone we can trust!"

"What do you say, Tyrus? Is it ready to hatch?" asked Daniel.

"Oh, uh, hum," muttered Tyrus. He placed his hand on top of the egg and thought for a moment. "No. That which lies within still slumbers."

"How can you tell?" challenged Lydia.

"I just know," said Tyrus. "I always knew when there was life in a Hota egg."

"Well, all right, I guess," Lydia said. "Let's go see what there is to see. Maybe we'll find some birds' eggs or mushrooms, or maybe even some honey. Max would like that.

"Why don't you come with us, Tyrus? You can stay in the shade," Lydia said, helping the old man to his feet.

"What about Max?" asked Daniel, pausing next to his sleeping brother.

"Let him sleep, he's still tired," said Lydia. "We'll be back before he even knows we're gone. We can surprise him with a treat in his bear bowl."

"That would be nice," said Daniel, smiling down. "Come on, let's go." And softly the three stole away, leaving the child and the egg beneath the tree.

Max could never quite remember what wakened him. He had been asleep, wrapped in some safe, pink and gold place, when a wonderful feeling crept over him. The cold grief that had numbed him since the death of his father and the dragon loosed its hold on him, receding from his heart like ice from the sun.

Tears of happiness trickled from his eyes as a small voice chimed in his mind, saying simply, "Now."

Max sat up, wiping his tears, and looked around him. He realized that the others were gone, but he was not afraid.

The egg sat on its cushion of dragonskin, lumpy blue and outwardly unchanged. But inside, something was happening. Max sat in front of the egg and wrapped his arms around his legs, hugging them tight to his chest. Smiling, he watched the egg and waited. Soon the spirit within the egg, which all along had spoken to and through him, would emerge.

The sun rose higher in the sky and the morning grew warmer. The birds continued to sing and the butterflies to dance, and the egg remained unchanged.

The sun beat down upon the waiting child and upon the lumpy blue egg, warming its shell and calling it to life.

Max sat up with a start at the very first noise and watched as the maze of cracks spread across the surface of the egg.

"Daniel! Lydia! Come back!" he cried, but there was no answer.

Then came a small crunching noise and a thick piece of shell dropped off the side of the egg. A small, pale blue muzzle probed the tiny opening and chewed on the edge of the shell.

"No!" cried Max, covering the hole with the palm of his hand. "Don't come out! It's not time yet! You can't come out, you've got to wait for Daniel. Or even Lydia. They'll know what to do! Please wait!"

Something touched his hand, nibbling softly, inquiring gently.

"Can you breathe? If I take my hand away will you promise to stay in there till Daniel gets back? Please, I'm not the one you want . . . really."

The soft thing withdrew from Max's hand. Fearing that he had cut off its air, Max quickly removed his hand and waited breathlessly for the little blue muzzle to return. But it didn't appear.

"Are you all right?" Max cried in alarm. Crouching on his hands and knees, he peered into the tiny hole, afraid of what he might find.

At first he saw nothing, and then he spied something blue.

Inside the egg, one small blue eye met his and his heart soared high and free and Max knew that he was no longer alone.

Calmly he settled back on his heels and watched the hole grow steadily larger.

As the sun neared its greatest height, the tiny blue creature freed itself at last from the shell. With small, uncertain gestures, it swayed back and forth. Cautiously it opened first one wet wing, then the other, and stood there wobbling unsteadily. The dragonling looked shyly at Max, and Max smiled down at it. It seemed quite right that he should reach in, pick the tiny thing up and place it gently on his arm.

They regarded each other for a long time, the tiny blue dragon and the small child, and each found the other perfect.

They were still sitting there, speaking without words, when the others returned.

"Oh, no!" gasped Daniel.

"Oh, Max! How could you! You did this on purpose!" yelled Lydia. Her cries trailed away and she stared at her brother with an odd expression. Somehow Max was different. He was still Max. That much was clear. There were his big ears sticking out like handles on a jug. The same big hazel eyes that were so often filled with tears. The same chubby cheeks and pointy chin. The same dirty fingers. But somehow he was different.

As she stared at her brother, resentment and anger churning in her stomach, she knew with a sad certainty that what had happened was right.

"I'm sorry," Max said softly. "I didn't mean for it to happen. I called you, but you didn't hear."

"That's all right, Max," Lydia heard herself say. "I don't mind."

"I'm glad," Max said with a shy smile. "I don't want you to be mad at me."

"I'm not," said Lydia as she bent to kiss his cheek, and to her surprise she found that it was true.

"So, you're to be Dragonlord, not me," Daniel said slowly. "I don't know what to think. What would Father say? Oh, why did I leave? I should have stayed here with the egg!"

"No," Tyrus said, shaking his head. "It would not have made any difference. This was no accident. It was meant to be."

"Maybe you're right," Daniel said in a low voice. "But it was expected of me and I gave Father my word. I've failed him."

"He would understand," Tyrus said. He wrapped his arm around Daniel's bowed shoulders. "Thee did thy duty and saw the egg and thy family to safety. The dragonling hatched and made its own choice. It would have been no different had thee been here. Can thee not see that they belong together?"

One quick glance was all that was needed to know that Tyrus was right.

"Now thee must assume a new role," said Tyrus.

"What?" Daniel said dejectedly.

"Protector," answered Tyrus. "Thee must be the strong arm that protects thy brother and the dragonling, for they are small and weak and will need thy strength to shield them from evil."

"What about me?" asked Lydia.

"Are thee not part of the whole?" asked Tyrus as he drew her near. "A strong arm needs a brain to guide it."

"I'm no dummy," said Daniel. "I can guide my own arm!"

"That's not what he means, Daniel," Lydia said softly. "He means that thinking's as important as fighting. And if we work together as a team, we'll be stronger."

"What do I do?" asked Max, scarcely raising his eyes from the dragon.

"Love," answered Tyrus. "Thee must love thy brother and sister and thy dragon as thee love thyself. For only then will thee be strong enough to survive the dangers that will surely come."

About the Author

Rose Estes began her life in a three-room apartment in Chicago which she shared with her mother, her father, her sister and a grandmother. Later the family moved to Houston.

Young Rose started reading at two and hasn't quit yet. Reading helped her survive (and almost enjoy) several major childhood illnesses. During one of them, which confined her to bed for more than a year, Rose created an imaginary world whose geography existed only on the folds of a quilt.

Since growing up, Rose Estes has traveled up to Alaska and down to Guatemala and seen most everything in between. She has lived in a log cabin in the mountains and in a driftwood house on a wild, remote ocean island. She has spent the night on top of an

Aztec pyramid and collected salamanders in a Mexican rain forest. She has been bitten by snakes in Mexico, Texas and Colorado.

Before turning to writing books, Rose Estes put in time as a hippie, a student, a newspaper reporter and an advertising copy writer. She is the author of numerous multiple-ending stories, including *Dungeons of Dread, Mountain of Mirrors* and six other best-selling titles in the Dungeons and Dragons® Endless Quest® line. *Children of the Dragon* is her first full-length novel.

Rose Estes now lives in Lake Geneva, Wisconsin, in a house that is older than she is. Living with her are her three children, a gang of cats and one slightly demented dog. She still likes to read best of all.